OPEN RANGE

Other Five Star Titles
by Zane Grey™:

Last of the Duanes (1996)
Rangers of the Lone Star (1997)
Woman of the Frontier (1998)
The Great Trek (1999)
The Westerners: Stories of the West (2000)
Rangle River: Stories of the West (2001)

OPEN RANGE

A Western Story

ZANE GREY™

Five Star • Waterville, Maine

Five Star First Edition Western Series.

Published in 2002 in conjunction with Golden West Literary
Agency.

Set in 11 pt. Plantin by Christina S. Huff.

Printed in the United States on permanent paper.

Library of Congress Cataloging-in-Publication Data

Grey, Zane, 1872–1939.
    Open range : a western story / by Zane Grey.
      p. cm.
    ISBN 0-7862-3260-9 (hc : alk. paper)
    1. New Mexico—Fiction. 2. Young men—Fiction. I. Title.
    PS3513.R6545 O64 2002
    813′.52—dc21   2001050171

OPEN RANGE

Editor's Note

The story, "Open Range," by Zane Grey first appeared as a five-part serial in the monthly magazine, *The Country Gentleman*, in the issues for March through July of 1927. This magazine was a publication of The Curtis Publishing Company, the same firm that also published *Ladies' Home Journal* and *The Saturday Evening Post*. Paramount Pictures had a long-standing agreement with Zane Grey to bring his stories to the screen and customarily would produce between four and five photoplays a year based on Zane Grey's fiction. Such a production schedule in time actually exceeded Zane Grey's ability to produce new stories fast enough. Any new story at which Grey was at work was usually submitted to Paramount before it was even offered to the magazine market. That was certainly the case with "Open Range." The film based on this story, titled BORN TO THE WEST (Paramount, 1926), was released eight months before the serial began appearing in *The Country Gentleman*. The staff screenwriter at Paramount who was assigned to adapt many of the Zane Grey literary properties was Lucien Hubbard. Since the previous year Paramount had already produced WILD HORSE MESA (Paramount, 1925), a story that dealt with rounding up wild horses, it is probable that Lucien Hubbard, who had adapted the earlier story, was asked to change the setting somewhat for "Open Range." It was changed, to the extent that it became a story about cattle rustling instead.

Probably because "Open Range" had not been used as the title for BORN TO THE WEST, it was therefore used the next year for a new Zane Grey film, OPEN RANGE (Paramount, 1927), with a story crafted from story elements in the serial that now had appeared under that title in *The Country Gentleman*. John Stone and J. Walter Reuben created the new screen adaptation. Since Zane Grey's contract with Paramount granted the film company only seven years to distribute any photoplay based on a Grey literary work, Paramount began exercising its right to produce remakes after the seventh year in the sound era during the 1930s. These films would naturally have different casts, but by adhering to the basic storylines of the originals some of the spectacular scenic footage could be used again, giving these films a production value on the screen that far exceeded what could be produced on the reduced budgets allotted for their production. BORN TO THE WEST (Paramount, 1926) starred Jack Holt and Raymond Hatton as the two men vying for the hand of Margaret Morris. In BORN TO THE WEST (Paramount, 1937) these rôles were assumed by John Wayne, John Mack Brown, and Marsha Hunt.

Harper & Bros., which had been Zane Grey's book publisher since 1910, only wanted to publish two Zane Grey novels a year and so could not really accommodate his expanded production of serials for Paramount and magazines in the 1920s, building up quite a backlog as a consequence. But it was as a result of this practice that the book publisher was able to continue publishing new Zane Grey books for nearly twenty years after the author's death in 1939. The paper shortage during the Second World War had caused Harper & Bros. to cut Zane Grey's THE GREAT TREK from 160,000 words to less than 60,000 words when it issued this book in

1943 under the title WILDERNESS TREK. Zane Grey's original manuscript was not restored until it appeared as THE GREAT TREK from Five Star Westerns in 1999. In 1947, when Harper & Bros. was interested in publishing "Open Range" as a book, the original magazine serial at under 50,000 words was thought to be too short for a novel. Therefore, Romer Grey, Zane Grey's elder son and then president of Zane Grey, Inc., hired a ghost writer to expand "Open Range" to more than 80,000 words, titling it VALLEY OF WILD HORSES (Harper, 1947). Most of this additional material consisted not of the profound descriptions of landscapes and settings that were so much a hallmark of Zane Grey's Western fiction, but was confined rather to elaborate psychological descriptions of what the characters were thinking and feeling.

OPEN RANGE, as it now appears in book form for the first time, is this story as Zane Grey originally wrote it, and, if it is a shorter book than Harper & Bros. wanted in 1947, the text is Zane Grey's from beginning to end. It is probably also worth adding that OPEN RANGE has never been filmed as Zane Grey wrote it.

Chapter One

The Panhandle was a lonely purple rangeland, unfenced and wind-swept. Bill Smith, cattleman, threw up a cabin and looked at the future with hopeful eyes. One day while plowing almost out of sight of his little home—which that morning he had left apprehensively owing to an impending event—he espied his wife Margaret coming along the edge of the plowed field. She had brought his lunch this day, despite his order to the contrary. Bill dropped the loop of his driving reins over the plow handle and strode toward her. Presently she sat down where the dark overturned earth met the line of bleached grass. Bill meant to scold Margaret for bringing his lunch, but it developed she had brought him something more. A son!

This son was born on the fragrant fresh soil, out on the open prairie, under the steely sun and the cool wind from off the Llano Estacado. He came into the world protesting against this primitive birth. Later, Bill often related that the youngster arrived squalling and showed that his lung capacity fitted his unusual size. Despite the mother's protests, Bill insisted on calling the lad Panhandle.

Panhandle early manifested a growing tendency toward self-assertion. He ran away from home. Owing to his short legs and scant breath he did not get very far down over the slope. His will and intention were tremendous. Did the dim desert heights call to the child? His parents had often seen him stand gazing into the purple distance. But Panhandle on this runaway occasion fell asleep on the dry grassy bottom of an irrigation ditch. By and by he was missed, and father and mother and the farm hands ran hither and thither in wild search for him. No one, however, found him. In the haste of the search someone left his work at the irrigation dam, and the water running down rudely awoke the child out of his dreams. Wet and bedraggled, squalling at the top of his lungs, Panhandle trudged back home to the relief of a distracted mother.

"Dog-gone it!" ejaculated Bill to his neighbors. "That kid's goin' to be just like me. I never could stay home."

A year later Bill Smith sold his farm and moved farther west in Texas, where he took up a homestead, and divided his time between that and work on a big irrigating canal that was being constructed.

Panhandle now lived on a ranch, and it was far lonelier than his first home because his father was away so much of the time. At first the nearest neighbor was Panhandle's uncle, who lived two long prairie miles away.

The boy undoubtedly had an adventuring soul. One day he discovered that a skunk had dug a hole under the front porch and had given birth to her kittens there. Panhandle was not afraid of them, and neither hurt nor frightened them. After a time he made playmates of them, and was one day hugely enjoying himself with them when his mother found him. She entreated Panhandle to let the little skunks alone. Panhandle would promise and then forget. His mother punished him, all to no avail. Then she adopted harsher measures.

Homesteaders had located near, and Mrs. Smith called on

them, in the hope that she could hire a cowboy or ranch hand to come over and destroy the skunks. It chanced there was no one but a Mrs. Hardman and her only boy. His name was Dick. He was seven years old, large for his age, a bold handsome lad with red hair. Mrs. Smith made a bargain with Dick, and led him back with her.

Here Panhandle took violent exception to having his pets killed or routed out by this boy he had never before seen. He did not like his looks anyway. But Dick paid little heed to Panhandle, except once when Mrs. Smith went into the house, and then he knocked Panhandle down. For once Panhandle did not squall. He got up, round-eyed, pale, with his hands clenched. He never said a word. Something was born in the depths of his gentle soul then.

Dick tore a hole in the little wall of rocks that supported the porch, and with a lighted torch on a stick he wormed his way in to rout out the skunks.

Panhandle suddenly was thrilled and frightened by a bellowing from Dick. The boy came hurriedly backing out of the hole. He fetched an odor with him that nearly suffocated Panhandle. Dick's eyes were shut. For the time being he had been blinded. He bounced around like a chicken with its head cut off, bawling wildly.

What had happened Panhandle did not know. But it certainly suited him. "Goody! Goody!" he shouted.

Then Panhandle saw smoke issuing from the hole under the porch. The mother skunk and her kittens scampered out into the weeds. He heard the crackle of flames. That boy had dropped his torch under the porch. Screaming, Panhandle ran to alarm his mother. But it was too late. There were no men near at hand, so nothing could be done. Panhandle stood crying beside his mother, watching their little home burn to the ground. Somehow in his mind the boy had been to blame. Panhandle peered around to find him, but he was gone. Never would Panhandle forget that boy.

They walked to the uncle's house and spent the night there. Soon another home was under construction on the same site. It was more of a shack than a house, for building materials were scarce, and the near approach of winter made hasty construction imperative. Winter came soon, and Panhandle and his mother were alone. It was cold; they huddled over the little wood fire. They had plenty to eat, but were very uncomfortable in the one-room shack. Bill Smith came home but seldom. That fall the valley had been overrun with homesteaders—nesters, they were called—and these newcomers passed by often from the town, drunk and rough.

Panhandle used to lie awake a good deal. During these lonely hours the moan of the prairie wind, the mourn of wolves, and yelp of coyotes became part of his existence. He understood why his mother barred and blocked the one door, placed the axe by the bed and the gun under her pillow. Even then he longed for the time when he would be old enough and big enough to protect her.

The lonely winter, with its innumerable hours of solitude for Mrs. Smith and the boy, had incalculable influence upon his character. She taught him much, in ways and things, words and feelings that became an integral part of his life.

At last the long winter ended, and, as spring advanced, a new and fascinating game came into Panhandle's life. It was to sit at the one little window and watch the cowboys ride by. How he came to worship them. They were on their way to the spring roundups. His father had told him all about them. Panhandle would strain his eyes to get a first glimpse of them, to count the shaggy prancing horses, the lithe supple riders with their great sombreros, their bright scarves, guns and chaps, and boots and spurs. Their lassoes. How they fascinated Panhandle. Ropes to whirl and throw at a running steer! That was a game he resolved to play when he grew up. And his mother, discovering his interest, made him a little reata and taught him how to throw it, how to make loops and knots. She told him how her people had owned horses, thrown lassoes, run cattle.

These were full days for the lad, rousing in him wonder and awe, eagerness and fear—strange longings for he knew not what.

Then one day his father brought home a black pony with three white socks and a white spot on his face. Panhandle was stricken with rapture. For him! He could have burst for very joy, but he could not speak. It developed that his mother would not let him ride the pony except when she led it. This roused as great a grief as possession was joy.

One day he stole Curly, and led him out of sight behind the barn, and, mounting him, rode down to the spring. Panhandle found himself alone. He was free. He was on the back of a horse. Mighty and incalculable fact!

Curly felt the spirit of that occasion. After drinking at the spring, he broke into a lope. Panhandle stuck on somehow and turned the pony toward the house. Curly loped faster. Panhandle felt the wind in his hair. He bounced up and down. Squealing with delight, he twisted his hands in the flowing mane and held on. At the top of the hill his joy became divided by fear. Curly kept on loping down the hill toward the house. Faster and faster! Panhandle bounced higher and higher, up on his neck, back on his haunches, until suddenly his hold broke and he was thrown. Down he went with a *thud*. It jarred him so he could hardly get up, and he reeled dizzily. There stood his mother, white of face, reproachful of eye. "Oh, Mama . . . I ain't hurt!" he cried.

Bill Smith was approached about this and listened, stroking his lean chin, while the mother eloquently enlarged upon the lad's guilt.

"Wal, wife, let the boy ride," he replied. "He's a nervy kid. You named him well. He'll make a great cowboy. Panhandle Smith. Pan, for short."

Pan heard that, and his heart beat high. How he loved his dad then! Cowboy meant one of the great riders of the range. He would be one. Thereafter he lived on the back of Curly. He learned to ride, to stick on like a burr, to keep his seat on the bare back of the pony, to move with him as he moved.

Pan was not quite six years old when he rode to his first roundup, which occurred that summer early in June. These genial fiery young men, lithe and tall and round-limbed, breathing the life and spirit of the range, crowded around Pan, proving that there never was a cowboy who did not like youngsters.

When the roundup began, he found that he was far from forgotten.

"Come on, Pan!" shouted one. "Ride in heah an' help me. Turn 'em back, kid."

Pan rode like the wind, breathless and radiant, beside himself with bliss.

Then another rider would yell to him: "Charge him, cowboy! Fetch him back."

And Pan, scarcely knowing what he was doing, saw with wild eyes how the yearling or calf would seem to be driven by him. There was always a cowboy near him, riding fast, yet close, yelling to him, making him a part of the roundup.

At the noon hour an older man, no doubt the rancher who owned the cattle, called off the work. A lusty voice from somewhere yelled: "Come an' git it!"

The rancher, espying Pan, rode over to him and said:

"Stranger, did you fetch your chuck with you?"

"No . . . sir," faltered Pan. "My mama . . . said for me to hurry back."

"Wal, you stay an' eat with me," replied the man kindly. "Shore them varmints might stampede, an' we'd need you powerful bad."

Pan sat next this big black-eyed man, in the circle of hungry cowboys. They made no more fun of Pan. He was one of them. Hard, indeed, was it for him to sit cross-legged, after the fashion of cowboys, with a steady plate upon his knees. But he had no trouble disposing of the juicy beefsteak and boiled potatoes and beans and hot biscuits Tex, the boss, piled upon his plate.

After dinner the cowboys resumed work.

"Stand heah by the fire, kid," Tex said to the boy.

Then Pan saw a calf being dragged across the ground. A mounted cowboy held the rope.

"The brand!" he yelled.

Pan stood there, trembling, while one of the flankers went down the tight rope to catch the bawling, leaping calf. Its eyes stood out; it foamed at the mouth. The flanker threw it over his leg on its back with hoofs sticking up. A brander with white iron leaped close. The calf bellowed. There was a sizzling of hair, a white smoke, the odor of burned hide, all of which sickened Pan.

Chapter Two

So this was how Panhandle Smith, at the mature age of five, received the stimulus that set the current of his life in one strong channel.

He called himself Tex. If his mother forgot to use this thrilling name, he was offended. He adopted Tex's way of walking, riding, talking. And all the hours of daylight, outdoors and indoors, he played roundup. At night his dreams were full of cowboys, chuck wagons, pitching horses, and bawling steers.

One by one pioneers came in their covered wagons to this promising range and took up homesteads of one-hundred-and-sixty acres each. Some of these men, like Pan's father, had to work part of the time away from home, to earn much-needed money.

Jem Blake, the latest of these incoming settlers, had chosen a site down in a deep swale that Pan always crossed when he went to visit his uncle. It was a pretty place, with grass and cottonwoods, and a thin stream of water, a lonesome and hidden spot that other homesteaders had passed by.

Pan met Jem one day and rode with him. He was a young man, pleasant and jolly, a farmer and would-be rancher, without any of the signs of cowboy about him. Pan thought this a great detriment, but he managed to like Jem, and loftily acquainted him with his achievements on Curly.

One day Pan saw Jem's wife, a pretty blonde-haired girl, strong and healthy and rosy-cheeked. Her sleeves were rolled up, showing round bare arms. Her smile won Pan, yet he was too shy to go in and get the cookies she offered.

Autumn days came, full and gray, with cold wind sweeping the plain, and threatening clouds lodging against the mountain peaks. Another winter was coming. Pan hated the thought. Snow, ice, piercing winds would prevent him from riding Curly. His father and mother wanted him to go with them to the settlement, one Saturday, for winter supplies. Pan's yearning for adventure almost persuaded him, but he preferred to stay with Curly. His mother demurred, but his father said he might remain at home.

"Pan, you ride over to Uncle George's with some things. But be careful not to get caught in a storm."

Thus it came about that Pan found himself alone for the first time in his life, master of himself, free to act as he chose.

And he did not choose to go at once to Uncle George's. His uncle was nice, but did not accord Pan the freedom he craved. So what with one and another of his important cowboy tasks the hours flew, and it was late before he got started across the prairie toward his uncle's homestead.

Pan never needed an excuse to ride fast, but now he had one that justified him. The two miles would not take long. He would have to hurry, for, indeed, it looked as if a storm were sweeping down from the black peaks. Pan realized that he should have gotten his errand done earlier in the day.

The cold wind stung his face and made his eyes water. Curly loped at his easy swift stride over the well-trodden trail. The bleached grass waved, the tumbleweeds rolled along the brown ground. There was no sun. All the west was draped in drab clouds.

Once across the swale where Blake lived, he brought Curly
to a gallop and soon reached Uncle George's place. No one at
home! Pan left his package and went on. As he trotted past
the Blake gate, Pan heard a sound. It startled him. Reining
Curly, he listened attentively. Blake's cabin stood back out of
sight among the dark woods. The barn, however, with its low
open-sided shed stood just inside the gate. The cows had
been brought in for milking. A lusty calf was trying to steal
milk from its mother. Chickens were going to roost. Pan did
not believe that any of these had made the call. He was about
to ride on by when suddenly he again caught a strange cry
that appeared to come from the barn or shed. It excited rather
than frightened him. Sliding off Curly, he pushed open the
big board gate and ran in.

Under the open shed he found Mrs. Blake, lying on some
hay that evidently she had just pulled down from the loft.
When she saw Pan, her pale convulsed face changed
somehow. "Oh, thank God!" she cried.

"Are you hurted?" asked Pan in hurried sympathy.

"No, but I'm in terrible pain."

"Aw . . . you're sick?"

"Yes. And I'm alone. Will you please . . . go for your
mother?"

"Mama an' Daddy went to town," replied Pan in distress.
"An' nobody is home at Uncle George's."

"Then you must be a brave little man and help me."

Bill Smith, hurrying homeward with his wife and Jem
Blake, was belated by the storm. It was midnight when they
arrived at Bill's house. They found Curly with bridle
hanging, standing in the snow beside the barn. Mrs. Smith
was distracted. Bill and Jem, although worried, did not fear
the worst. With lanterns they set out upon the tracks Curly

had left in the snow. Bill's wife would not remain behind.

Soon they arrived at Blake's homestead, although the pony tracks became difficult to follow, and found Pan wide-awake, huddled beside the cow, true to the trust that had been given him. Mrs. Blake was not in bad condition, considering the circumstances, nor was the baby. It was a girl, which Jem named Lucy right then and there, after his wife.

The men carried the mother and her babe up to the house, while Mrs. Smith followed with the now sleepy Pan. They built fires in the open grate and in the kitchen stove, and left Mrs. Smith to attend to the mother. Both women heard the men talking. But Pan never heard, for he had been put to bed in a corner, rolled in blankets.

"Dog-gone my hide!" exclaimed Bill. "Never seen the beat of that kid of mine!"

"Mebbe Pan saved both their lives, God bless him," replied Blake.

"*¿Quién sabe?* It might be. . . . Wal, strange things happen. Jem, that kid of mine was born right out on the plowed field. An' here comes your kid . . . born in the cow shed on the hay!"

"It is strange," mused Blake, "though we ought to look for such happenin's out in this great West."

"Wal, Pan an' Lucy couldn't have a better birthright. It ought to settle them two kids for life."

"You mean grow up an' marry some day? Shake on it, Bill."

The winter passed for Pan much as had the preceding one, except that he had more comfort to play his everlasting game of roundup.

"When will Lucy be big enough to play with me?" he often asked. The strange little baby girl had never passed from his mind, although he had never seen her. She seemed to form the third link in his memory of the forging of his life. Curly . . . the cowboys . . . and Lucy!

At last the snow melted, the prairie took on a sheen of green, the trees burst into bud, and birds returned to sing once more. Then there came the fourth epoch in Pan's life. His father brought him a saddle. It was far from new, of Mexican make, covered with rawhide, and had an enormous shiny horn. Pan loved it almost as much as he loved Curly.

The fifth, and surely the greatest event in Pan's rapidly developing career, although he did not know it then, was when his mother took him over to see his baby, Lucy Blake. It appeared that the parents in both homesteads playfully called her "Pan's Baby."

Pan's first sight of Lucy was when she crawled over the floor to get to him. She was dressed in a little white dress. Her feet and legs were chubby. She had tiny pink hands. Her face was like a wild rose dotted with two violets for eyes. And her hair was spun gold. Marvelous as were all these things they were as nothing to the light of her smile. Pan's shyness vanished, and he sat on the floor to play with her.

Every Sunday that summer the Smiths visited at the homestead of the Blakes. They became fast friends. Pan never missed one of these visits, and the time came when he rode over on his own account. Lucy was the most satisfactory cowgirl in all the world.

Meanwhile the weeks and months passed, and the number of homesteaders increased, more and more cattle dotted the range. When winter came, some of the homesteaders, including Pan and his mother, moved into Littletown to send their children to school.

Pan's first teacher was Emma Jones. He liked her immediately, which was when she called to take him to school.

21

Dick Hardman came again into Pan's life, fatefully, inevitably, as if the future had settled something inscrutable and sinister, and childhood days, school days, days of youth and manhood had been inextricably planned before they were born. Dick was in a higher grade. He had grown into a large boy, handsomer, bolder, with a mop of red hair that shown like a flame. He called Pan "the little skunk tamer," and incited other boys to ridicule. So the buried resentment in Pan's depths smoldered and burst into blaze again.

Then the endless school days were over for a while. Summer had come. Pan moved back to the beloved homestead, to the open ranges, to Curly and Lucy. Only she had changed. She could stand at his knee and call him Tex.

Another uncle had moved into the country to take up a homestead. Pan now had a second place to ride to, farther away, over a wilder bit of range, and much to his liking. He saw cowboys every time he rode there.

One day while Pan was at his new uncle's, a dreadful thing happened—the first real tragedy. Some cowboy left the slide door of the granary open. Curly got in there at the wheat. Before it became known, he ate enormously and then drank copiously. It foundered him. It killed him.

When Pan came out of his stupefaction to realize his actual loss, he was heartbroken. He could not be consoled. Hours he spent crying over his saddle.

That autumn the homesteaders erected a schoolhouse of their own. It was scarcely three miles from Pan's home.

"Pan, can you walk it?" asked Bill Smith with his keen eye on the lad.

"Yes, Daddy . . . but . . . but . . . ," replied Pan.

"A-huh. An' before long Lucy will be old enough to go, too," added his father. "Reckon you'll take her?"

"Yes, Daddy." And for Pan there was real gladness in that promise.

"Wal, you're a good boy," declared his father. "An' you won't have to walk to school. I've traded for two horses for you."

"Two!" screamed Pan, wild with joy.

In due time the new horses arrived at the Smith homestead. Their names were Pelter and Pilldarlick. Pelter was a pinto, snappy and pretty, although he had a wicked eye. Pilldarlick was not showy, but was much better than he looked, and soon filled the void in Pan's heart.

Pan was the proud cynosure of all eyes as he rode Pilldarlick around the yard for the edification of his schoolmates. It was the happiest day of Pan's life—until Dick Hardman arrived on a spirited little black mustang.

"Hey, where'd you git that nag?" Dick yelled when he sighted Pan. "An' say, your saddle ain't nothin' but rawhide on a stump."

"You're a liar!" shouted Pan, fiercely tumbling off Pilldarlick.

The red-headed lad pitched out of his saddle and made for Pan.

They began to fight. Instinct was Pan's guide. He hit and scratched and kicked. But Dick, being the larger, began to get the better of the battle, and soon was beating Pan badly when the new teacher came to his rescue.

Chapter Three

Recess came. Before half the scholars were out of the room, Dick and Pan had run to the barn, out of the teacher's sight, and here they fell upon each other like wildcats. It did not take Dick long to give Pan the first real beating of his life. Cut lip, bloody nose, black eye, dirty face, torn shirt—these things betrayed Pan at least to Miss Hill. She kept him in after school, and, instead of scolding, she talked sweetly and kindly. Pan came out of his sullenness, and felt love for her rouse in him. But somehow he could not promise not to fight again.

"S'pose Dick Hardman does that all over again?" Pan expostulated in despair. "What'll my . . . my . . . Daddy . . . say when he hears I got licked!" he sobbed.

She compromised finally by accepting Pan's willing promise not to pick a fight with Dick.

Despite the unpleasant proximity of Dick, that winter at school promised to be happy and helpful to Pan. There were three large boys, already cowboys, who attended Miss Hill's school. Pan gravitated at once to them, and to his great satisfaction they accepted him.

Swiftly that winter passed. Pan had a happy growing time of it. Study had not seemed so irksome, perhaps owing to the fact that he had a horse and saddle; he could ride to and fro; he often stopped to see Lucy, who was now big enough to want to go to school herself; and the teacher had won his love. Pan kept out of fights with Dick Hardman until one recess when Dick called him "teacher's pet." That inflamed Pan, as much because of the truth of it as the shame. So this time, although he had hardly picked a fight, he was the first to strike. With surprising suddenness he hit the big Dick square on the nose. When Dick got up howling and swearing, his face was hideous with dirt and blood. Then began a battle that dwarfed the one in the barn. Pan had grown considerably. He was quick and strong, and, when once his mother's fighting blood burned in him, he was as fierce as a young savage. But again Dick whipped him.

Spring came with roundups too numerous for Pan to keep track of. And a swift happy summer sped by.

Pan grew tall and supple, with promise of developing the true horseman's build. Then the spring arrived when he was twelve years old and his father consented to let him ride for wages at the roundup.

He joined a big outfit. There were over fifty cowboys, two bed wagons, two chuck wagons, and strings of horses too numerous to count. A new horse to ride twice a day! This work was as near paradise as Pan felt he had ever been. But for one circumstance it would have been absolutely perfect, and that was that he had no boots. Fast-riding cowboy without boots!

That roundup was prolific of wonderful experiences. One night when a storm threatened, the foreman called to the cowboys not on duty: "Talk to 'em low, boys, fer they're gettin' ready."

He meant that the herd of cattle was likely to stampede. And when the thunder and rain burst, the herd broke away with a trampling roar. Pan got soaked to the skin and lost in the rain. When he returned to camp, only the cook and wagons were there. Next morning the cowboys straggled in bunches, each driving part of the stampeded herd.

Pan never forgot Lucy's first day of school when he rode over with her sitting astride behind him, "ringin' his neck," as a cowboy remarked. Pan had not particularly been aware of that part of the performance, for he was used to having Lucy cling to him. That embarrassed him. He dropped her off rather unceremoniously at the door and went to put his horse in the corral. She was little and he was big, which fact further bore upon his consciousness through the giggles of the girls and gibes of the boys. But they did not make any change in his attitude toward Lucy. All winter he took her to and from school on his horse. The summer following he worked for his uncle.

As Pan grew older, time seemed so much shorter than when he was little. There was so much to do. And all at once he was fifteen years old. His mother gave him a party on that birthday, which was marked on his memory by the adulation his boy friends paid to Lucy. She was by far the prettiest girl in the valley. He did not know exactly what to make of his resentment, nor of the queer attitude of proprietorship he had assumed over her.

He was destined to learn more about his state of mind. It happened the next day at school during the noon hour. That late November a spell of Indian summer weather had lingered, and the pupils ate their lunches out under the trees.

Suddenly Lucy came running up to Pan, who as usual was having to care for his horse. Her golden hair was flying, disheveled. She was weeping. Her big violet eyes streamed with tears.

"Pan . . . you go right off . . . and thrash Dick Hardman!" she cried passionately.

"Lucy . . . what's he done?" queried Pan, after a sudden sense of inward shock.

"He's always worrying me . . . when you're not around. I never told 'cause I knew you'd fight. . . . But now he done it. He grabbed me and kissed me! Before all the boys!"

Pan looked steadily at her tear-wet face, seeing Lucy differently. She was not a baby any more. For some strange reason beyond his understanding he was furious with her. Pushing her aside, he strode toward the group of boys, leering close by.

Dick Hardman, a strapping big lad now, edged back into the crowd. Pan violently burst into it, forcing the boys back, until he confronted his adversary. On Dick's sallow face the brown freckles stood out prominently. Something in the look and advance of Pan had intimidated him. But he blustered, he snarled.

"You're a skunk," Pan said fiercely, and struck out with all his might.

The fight that ensued was no boyish conflict, but a grim, desperate, relentless battle that at the end found Pan bruised, torn, and bleeding, yet the victor over his larger opponent.

Chapter Four

They did not meet again during the winter. It was a hard winter, and Pan left school and stayed close to home, working for his mother, and playing less than at any time before.

"I heard Dick say he'd kill you someday," said one cowboy seriously. "An' take it from me, kid, he's a bad *hombre*."

"A-huh!" was all the reply Pan vouchsafed as he walked away. He did not like to be reminded of Dick. It sent an electric spark to the deep-seated, smoldering mine in his breast.

When springtime came, Pan joined the roundup in earnest, for part of the cattle outfit now belonged to his father. Out on the range the forty riders waited for the wagons. There were five cowboys from Big Sandy in Pan's bunch, and several more arrived from the Crow Roost country. Old Dutch John, a famous range character, was driving the chuck wagon.

Next day the outfit rode the west side of Dobe Creek, rounding up perhaps a thousand cattle. Pete Blaine and Hooley roped calves while Pan helped hold up.

On the following day the riders circled Blue Lakes, where cattle swarmed.

These two lakes were always dry, except during the spring; now they were full, with green grass blanketing the range as far as eye could see. By Monday long lines of cattle moved with flying dust down to the spot chosen for the roundup. As the herds closed in, the green range itself seemed to be moving. When thrown together all these cattle formed a sea of red and white. It looked impossible to separate cows and calves from the others. But dozens of fearless cowboys soon began to cut out the cows and calves.

It was a spectacle that inspired Pan as never before. The wagons were lined up near the lake, their big white canvas tops shining in the afternoon sun, and higher on a bench stood the "hoodlum" or bed wagon, so stocked with bedrolls that it resembled a haystack. Beyond the margin of the lake four hundred fine saddle horses grazed, and kicked, and bit at one another. Beyond the saddle horses grazed the day herd of cattle. And over on the other side dinned the mêlée over the main herd, the incessant riding, yelling of the cowboys, and the bawling of the cows.

When all the cows and calves were cut out, a rider of each outfit owning cattle on that range would go through to claim those belonging to his brand. Next the herd of bulls and steers, old cows and yearlings, would be driven back out upon the range.

Fires were started, and, as there was no wood on that range, buffalo chips were used instead. It took many cowboys to collect sufficient for their needs.

Pan learned something from every cowboy he met, and it was not all for the best. That roundup was his real introduction to the raw range. When the time came for the outfit to break up, with each unit taking its own cattle, the boss said to Pan: "Come ride fer me."

Pan flushed and pleased, mumbled his thanks, but he had to work for his father.

That fall Jem-Blake sold his farm, and took his family to New Mexico. He had not been prospering in the valley, and things had gone from bad to worse. Pan did not get home in time to say good bye to Lucy—something that hurt in an indefinable way. He had not forgotten Lucy, but in his mind she had become a steadfast factor in his home life. She left a little note of farewell, simple and loyal, hopeful, yet somehow stultified.

The Hardmans had also moved away from the valley—where? none of the neighbors appeared to know. But Pan was assured of two facts concerning them; namely, that Dick had gotten into a serious shooting scrape in which he had wounded a rancher's son, and, secondly, that from some unknown source the Hardmans had acquired or been left some money.

Pan promptly forgot his boyhood enemy. This winter was the last that he spent at home. He rode the Limestone range that summer and, according to cowboys' gossip, was fast developing all the qualities that pertained to the best riders of the day.

Upon returning home, he found that his father had made unwise deals and was not getting along very well. Grasping settlers had closed in on the range. Rustlers had ridden down from the north, raiding the valley. During Pan's absence a little sister was born. As he played with the baby, he was reminded of Lucy. What had become of her? It occurred to Pan that sooner or later he must hunt her up.

Pan decided that he could not remain idle during the winter. So he decided to join two other adventurous cowboys who had planned to go south, and, in the spring, come back with some of the great herds being driven north.

But Pan liked the vast ranges of the Lone Star State, and he rode there for two years, inevitably drifting into the wild free life of the cowboys. Sometimes he sent money home to his mother, but that was seldom, because he was always in debt. She wrote him regularly, which fact was the only link between him and the old home memories. Thoughts of Lucy returned now and then on the lonely rides on night watches, and it seemed like a sweet melancholy dream. Never a word did he hear of her.

Spring had come again when he rode into the Panhandle, and, as luck would have it, he fell in with an outfit that was driving cattle to Montana, a job that would take until late fall. To his chagrin, stories of his wildness had preceded him. Ill rumor traveled swiftly. Pan was the more liked and respected by these riders. But he feared gossip of the southern ranges would reach his mother. He would go home that fall to reassure her of his well-being, and that he was not one of those "bad, gun-throwing cowboys."

But always he was drifting, with the swift months flying by as fleet as the mustangs he rode, and he did not reach home. The Cimarron, the Platte, the Arkansas ranges came to know the tracks of his horses and, after he had drifted on, to remember him as few cowboys were remembered.

At twenty years of age, Panhandle Smith looked older— looked the hard life, the hard fare, the hard companionship that had been his lot as an American cowboy. He had absorbed all the virtues of the remarkable character, and most of the vices. But he had always kept aloof from women. Pan never lost the reverence for women his mother had instilled in him, nor his first and only love for Lucy Blake.

One summer night Pan was standing night guard duty for his cowboy comrade, who was enamored of the daughter of the rancher for whom they worked. Many times Pan had ridden and worked with a boy afflicted with a similar malady.

This night, however, Pan had been conscious of encroaching melancholy. Perhaps it was a yearning for something he did not know how to define.

The range spread away dark, lonely, and wild. No wind

stirred. The wolves and coyotes were quiet. All at once the whole world seemed empty to Pan. It was an unaccountable feeling. The open range, the solitude, the herd of cattle in his charge, the comrades asleep, the horses grazing around their pickets—these always sufficient things suddenly lost their magic potency. He divined at length that he was homesick. And by the time the watch was ended he had determined to quit his job and ride home.

Chapter Five

He reached Littletown at dark. It had grown to be a sizable settlement. Pan treated himself to a room at the new hotel and, after supper, went out to find somebody he knew.

It was Saturday night, and the town was full of riders and ranchers. He expected to meet an old acquaintance any moment, but to his surprise he did not. Finally he went to Campbell's store. John Campbell did not recognize him.

"Howdy, stranger, reckon you've got the best of me," he replied to Pan's question, and he sized up the tall lithe rider.

"Now, John, you used to give me a stick of candy every time I came to town," said Pan with a laugh.

"Wal, I done that for every Tom, Dick, an' Harry of a kid in this hyar country," returned the old man, stroking his beard. "But durn if I recollect you."

"Panhandle Smith," announced Pan.

"Wal, Pan, if it ain't you, by gosh!" Campbell ejaculated cordially. "But no one here will ever recognize you. Say, you've sprung up. We've heerd a lot about you . . . nothin' of late years, though, now I tax myself. Cowboy, you've seen some range life, if talk is true."

"You mustn't believe all you hear, Mister Campbell," replied Pan with a smile. "I'd like to know about my dad and mother."

"Wal, haven't you heard?" queried Campbell hesitatingly.

"What?" flashed Pan, noting the other's sudden change to gravity. "It's two years and more since I got a letter from Mother."

"You ought to have come home long ago," Campbell said. "Your father lost his cattle. Old deal with Hardman that stood for years. Mebbe you never knowed about it. There are ranchers around here who swear Hardman drove sharp deals. Wal, your father sold the homestead an' left. Reckon it's been over a year."

"Where'd they go?"

"Your pa never told me where, but I heerd afterward that he hit Hardman's trail an' went to western New Mexico. Marco is the name. New country up there. Gold an' silver minin', some cattle outfits goin' in, an' lately I heerd of some big wild hoss deals on."

"Well!" exclaimed Pan, in profound amaze and sorrow at this news. "Why did Dad go?"

"Reckon I couldn't say for sure. But he was sore at Hardman, an' the funny thing is he wasn't sore till some time after Hardman left these parts. Mebbe he learned somethin'. An' you can learn whatever it was, if you hunt up them ranchers who once got stung by Hardman."

"A-huh," Pan muttered thoughtfully. "Don't know as I care to learn. Dad will tell me. Jem Blake, now, what become of him?"

"Jem, a while back, I reckon some years, though, after you left home, was foreman for Hardman's outfit. An' he went to Marco first. Reckon Hardman sent him up there to scout around."

"Marco. How do you get there?"

"Wal, it's on the old road to Californy."

Pan went to the seclusion of his room, and there in the dark, sleepless, he knew the pangs of remorse. Without real-

34

izing the flight of years, always meaning to return home, to help father, mother, little sister, to take up again with his never-forgotten Lucy—he had allowed the wild life of the range to hold him too long.

Next day Pan sold his outfit, except the few belongings he cherished, and boarded a westbound stage. Once on the way he recovered from his brooding mood and gradually awakened to the fact that he was riding to a new country, a new adventure—the biggest of his life—in which he must make amends to his mother, and to Lucy.

Riding by stage was not new to Pan, although he had never before taken more than a day's journey. The stage driver, Jim Wells, was an old-timer. He had been a pony express rider, miner, teamster and freighter, and now, grizzled and scarred, he liked to perch upon the driver's seat of the stage, chew tobacco, and talk. His keen eyes took Pan's measure in one glance.

"Pitch your bag up, cowboy, an' climb aboard," he said. "An' what might your handle be?"

"Panhandle Smith," replied Pan nonchalantly, "late of Sycamore Bend."

"Wal, now, whar'd I hear thet name? I got a plumb good memory fer names an' faces. 'Pears I heerd that name in Cheyenne, last summer. I got it. Cowpuncher named Panhandle rode downstreet, draggin' a bolt of red calico thet unwound an' stampeded all the hosses. Might thet lad have happened to be you?"

"I reckon it might," Pan replied with a grin. "But if you know any more about me, keep it under your sombrero."

"Haw! Haw!" roared Wells, slapping his knee. "By golly, I will if I can. There's a funny old lady inside what's powerful afeerd of bandits, an' there's a gurl. I seen her takin' in your size an' spurs, an' thet gun you pack sort of comfortable-like.

An' there's a gambler, too, if ever I saw one. Reckon I'm goin' to enjoy this ride."

After the next stop, when the travelers got dinner, Pan returned to the stage to find a young lady perched upon the driver's seat. She had serious gray eyes and pale cheeks.

"I took your seat," she said shyly, "but there's enough room."

"Thanks, I'll ride inside," replied Pan.

"But if you don't sit here . . . someone else might . . . and I . . . he . . . ," she faltered, flushing a little.

"Oh, in that case, I'll be glad to," Pan interrupted, and climbed to the seat beside her. He had become aware of the appearance of a flashily dressed, hawk-eyed individual about to enter the stage. "Are you traveling alone?"

"No, thank you. Father is with me, but he never sees anything. I have been annoyed," she replied.

The stage driver arrived, and surveyed the couple on the seat with a wink and a grin and a knowing look.

The little lady rode three whole days on the driver's seat between Pan and Wells. She made the hours fleet. When the stage reached Las Vegas, she got off with her father and turned in the crowd to wave good bye. Her eyes were wistful with what might have been. They haunted Pan.

As the days passed, the numbers of wild horses increased until they ran into the thousands. Horses had meant more to Pan than anything. If he had ridden these desert ranges, he would inevitably have become permanently a hunter and lover of wild horses.

Western New Mexico at last! It appeared a continuation and a magnifying of all the color and wildness and vastness. Sand dunes and wastes of black lava, dry lake beds, and cone-shaped extinct volcanoes, with the ragged crater-mouths gaping, low ranges of yellow cedar-dotted hills, valleys of purple and green forests on the mountain slopes—all these in endless variety were new to the cowboy of the plains. The homesteader, that hopeful and lonely pioneer, was as scarce as the streams.

One night, hours after dark, the stage rolled into Marco, with Pan one of five passengers. Marco! How unusual the swelling of his heart. The long three-weeks' ride had ended. The stage rolled down a main street the like of which Pan had never even imagined. It was crude, rough, garish with lights and stark board fronts of buildings, and a motley jostling crowd of men; women, too, were not wanting in the throngs streaming up and down. It was Saturday night. Noise and dust filled the air.

If Pan had not been keenly strung, after long weeks, with the thought of soon seeing his mother, father, his little sister, and Lucy, he would yet have been excited over this adventure beyond the Rockies.

Contrary to his usual habit of spending his money like most cowboys spent it, which was throwing it to the winds, he had exercised rigid economy on this trip. He had between four and five hundred dollars. There was no telling in what difficulties he might find his father. So Pan took cheap lodgings, and patronized a restaurant kept by a Chinaman.

He chose a table at which sat a young man whose face and hands and clothes told of rough life in the open, in contact with elemental things.

"Mind if I sit here?" Pan asked.

"Help yourself, stranger," was the reply, accompanied by an appraising glance from level quiet eyes.

"I'm sure hungry. How's the chuck here?" went on Pan.

"The chink is a first-rate cook an' clean. . . . Just come to town?"

37

"Yes," replied Pan. "And it took a darn' long ride to get here. From Texas."

"That so? Well, I come from western Kansas, just across the Colorado line."

"Been here long?"

"Reckon a matter of six months."

"What's your work, if you'll excuse curiosity. I'm green, you see, and want to know."

"I've been workin' a minin' claim. Gold."

"A-huh!" replied Pan with quickened interest. "Sounds awful good to me. I never saw any gold but a few gold eagles, and they've sure been scarce enough."

Pan's frankness, and that something simple and careless about him, combined with his appearance always created the best of impressions upon men.

His companion grinned across the table as if he had shared Pan's experience. "Reckon you needn't tell me you're a cowpuncher. I heard you comin' before I saw you. My name's Brown . . . Charley Brown."

"Howdy, glad to meet you," replied Pan, and then with evident hesitation: "Mine is Smith."

"Panhandle Smith?" queried the other.

"Why, sure," returned Pan with a laugh.

"Shake," was the reply Brown made.

"I'm 'most as lucky as I am unlucky," Pan said warmly. "It's a small world. Now tell me, Brown, have you seen or heard anything of my dad, Bill Smith?"

"No, sorry to say. But I haven't mingled much. Been layin' pretty low, because the fact is I think I've struck a rich claim. An' it's made me cautious."

"A-huh. Pretty wide-open town, I'll bet. I appreciate your confidence in me."

"To tell you the truth I'm darn' glad to run into someone I

like the looks of. Lord, I wish I could have my wife an' baby here."

"Married, and got a kid. That's fine. But it must be tough to be separated from your family. I'm not married, but I know what a little girl means. . . . Say, Brown, did you ever run into a man out here named Jem Blake?"

"No."

"Or a man named Hardman? Jard Hardman?"

"Hardman! Now you're talkin', Panhandle. I should smile I have." The one word Hardman had struck fire from this young miner.

"What's Hardman doing?" asked Pan quietly.

"Everything, an' between you an' me, he's doin' every-body. Jard Hardman is in everything. Minin', ranchin', an' I've heard he's gone in for this wild horse chasin'. That's the newest boom around Marco. But Hardman has big interests here in town. It's rumored he's back of the Yellow Mine, the biggest saloon an' gamblin' hell in town."

"Well, I'll be dog-goned," ejaculated Pan thoughtfully. "Things turn out funny. You can show me that place presently. Does Hardman hang out here?"

"Part of the time. He travels to Frisco, Salt Lake, an' Saint Louis where he sells cattle an' horses. He has a big ranch out here in the valley, an' stays there some. His son runs the outfit."

"His son?" Pan queried, suddenly hot with a flash of memory.

"Yes, his son," replied Brown, eying Pan earnestly. "Reckon you must know Dick Hardman?"

"I used to . . . long ago," replied Pan.

"Old Hardman makes the money, an' Dick blows it in," went on Brown, with something of contempt in his voice. "Dick plays, an' they say he's a rotten gambler. He drinks like a fish, too. I heard he'd fetched a girl here from Frisco."

"A-huh! Well, that's enough about my old schoolmate, thank you," rejoined Pan. "Tell me, Brown, what's this Marco town anyway?"

"Well it's both old an' new," replied the other. "That's about all, I reckon. Gold an' silver strikes out in the hills have made a boom this last year or so. That's what fetched me. The town is twice the size it was when I saw it first, an' many times more people. There's a lot of the riff-raff that work these minin' towns. Gamblers, sharks, claim jumpers, outlaws, adventurers, tramps, an', of course, the kind of women that go along with them. A good many cow outfits make this their headquarters now. An' last, this horse tradin', an' wild horse catchin'. Sellin' an' shippin' has attracted lots of men. Everyday or so, a new fellar, like you, drops in from east of the Rockies. There are some big mining men investigatin' the claims. An' if good mineral is found, Marco will be solid, an' not just a mushroom town."

"Any law?" inquired Pan thoughtfully.

"Not so you'd notice it much, especially when you need it," Brown asserted grimly. "Matthews is the town marshal. Self-elected, so far as I could see. An' he's hand an' glove with Hardman. He's mayor, magistrate, sheriff, an' the whole caboodle, includin' the court. But there are substantial men here, who sooner or later will organize an' do things. They're too darned busy now, workin', gettin' on their feet."

"A-huh. I savvy. I reckon you're giving me a hunch that, in your private opinion, Matthews isn't exactly straight where some interests are concerned. Hardman's, for instance. I've run across that sort of deal in half a dozen towns."

"You got me," replied Brown soberly.

"Well, I was lucky to run into you," said Pan. "Now let's go out and see the town, especially the Yellow Mine."

Pan had visited some fairly wild and wide-open towns. But they had owed their wildness and excitement and atmosphere to the range and the omnipresent cowboy. Old-timers had told him stories of Abilene and Dodge, when they were in their heyday. He had gambled in Juárez, across the Texas border where there was no law. Some of the Montana cattle towns were far from slow. But here he sensed a new element. And soon he grasped it as the fever of the rush for gold.

The town appeared about a mile long, spread out on two sides of the main street, graduating from the big buildings of stone and wood in the center to flimsy frame structures and tents along the outskirts. Pan estimated that he must have passed three thousand people during his stroll, up one side of the street and down the other. The many yellow lights from open doors and windows fell upon the throngs moving to and fro.

Pan's guide eventually led him into the Yellow Mine. He saw a long wide room full of moving figures, thin wreaths of blue smoke that floated in the glaring yellow lights. A bar ran the whole length of this room, and drinkers were crowded in front of it. The *clink* of glass, the *clink* of gold, the increased murmur of hoarse voices almost drowned faint strains of music from another room that opened from this one.

The thousand and one saloons and gambling dives that Pan had seen could not in any sense compare with this one. This was on a big scale without restraint of law or order. Piles of gold and greenbacks littered the tables where roulette, faro, poker, were in progress. Black-garbed, pale, hard-faced gamblers sat with long mobile hands on the tables. Bearded men, lean-faced youths bent with intent gaze over their cards. Sloe-eyed Mexicans in their high-peaked sombreros and gaudy trappings lounged here and there, watching, waiting— for what did not seem clear to Pan. Drunken miners in their

41

shirt sleeves stamped through the open door, to or from the bar. Young women with bare arms and necks and painted faces were in evidence, some alone, most of them attended by men.

In one corner of the big room, almost an alcove, Pan espied a large round table at which were seated six players engrossed in a game of poker. He saw thousands of dollars in gold and notes on that table. A pretty, flashy girl with bold eyes and lazy sleepy smile hung over the shoulder of one of the gamblers.

Pan's comrade nudged him in the side. Brown was gazing with gleaming eyes at the young card player over whose shoulder the white-armed girl hung.

Then Pan saw a face that was strangely familiar—a handsome face of a complexion between red and white, with large sensual mouth, bold eyes, and a broad low brow. The young gambler was Dick Hardman.

Pan knew him. The recognition meant nothing, yet it gave Pan a start, a twinge, and then sent a slow heat along his veins. He laughed to find the boyishness of old still alive in him. After eight years of hard life on the range! By that sudden resurging of long-forgotten emotion Pan judged the nature of what the years had made him. It would be interesting to see how Dick Hardman met him.

But it was the girl who first seemed drawn by Pan's piercing gaze. She caught it—then looked a second time. Sliding off the arm of Hardman's chair, she moved with undulating motion of her slender form, and with bright eyes, around the table toward Pan. At that moment, Dick Hardman looked up from his cards and watched her.

Chapter Six

"Hello, cowboy. How'd I ever miss you?" she queried roguishly, running her bright eyes from his face down to his spurs and back again.

"Good evening, lady," replied Pan, removing his sombrero and bowing with his genial smile. "I just come to town."

She hesitated as if struck by a deference she was not accustomed to.

"Did you take off that big hat because you know you're mighty good to look at?" she asked archly.

"Well, no, hardly," answered Pan.

"What for then?"

"It's a habit I have when I meet a pretty girl."

"Thank you. Does she have to be pretty?"

"Reckon not. Any girl, miss."

"You *are* a stranger in Marco. Look out somebody doesn't shoot a hole in that hat when you doff it."

While she smiled up at him, losing something of the hawklike, possession-taking manner that had at first characterized her, Pan could see Dick Hardman staring hard across the table. Before Pan could find a reply for the girl, one of the gamesters addressed Hardman: "Say, air you playin' cairds or watchin' your dame make up to that big hat an' high boots?"

Pan grasped the opportunity, although he never would have let that remark pass under any circumstances. He disen-

43

gaged his right hand from the girl's, and, stepping up to the table, drawing her with him, he bent a glance upon the disgruntled gambler.

"Excuse me, mister," he began in the slow, easy, cool speech of a cowboy, "but did you mean me?"

His tone, his presence, drew the attention of all at the table, especially the one he addressed and Hardman. The former laid down his cards. Shrewd eyes took Pan's measure, surely not missing the gun at his hip.

"Suppose I mean you?" demanded the gambler curiously.

"Well, if you did, I'd have to break up your game," Pan replied apologetically. "You see, mister, it hurts my feelings to have anyone make fun of my clothes."

"All right, cowboy, no offense meant," returned the other, at which everyone except Hardman let out a laugh. "But you'll break up our game, anyhow, if you don't troop off with Louise there."

Dick stared insolently and fixedly at Pan. He appeared as much puzzled as annoyed. Manifestly he was trying to place Pan, and did not succeed. Pan had hardly expected to be recognized, although he stood there a moment, head uncovered, under the light, giving his old enemy eye for eye. In fact, his steady gaze disconcerted Dick, who turned his glance on the amused girl. Then his face darkened and he spat out his cigar to utter harshly: "Go on, you cat! And don't purr around me any more."

Insolently she laughed in his face. "You forget I can scratch." Then she drew Pan away from the table, beckoning for Brown to come, also. Halting presently near the wide opening into the dance hall, she said: "I'm always starting fights. What might your name be, cowboy?"

"I'll introduce you," drawled Brown. "Meet Panhandle Smith, from Texas."

"Well," she echoed musingly, fastening her hands in the lapels of his coat. "I thought you'd have a high-sounding handle. Will you dance with me?"

"Sure, but I'm afraid I step pretty high and wide."

They entered another garish room, around which a throng of couples spun and wagged and tramped and romped. Pan danced with the girl and, despite the jostling of the heavy-footed miners, acquitted himself in a manner he thought was creditable for him. He had not been one of the dancing cowboys.

"That was a treat after those clodhoppers," she said when the dance ended. "You're a modest boy, Panhandle. You've got me guessing. I'm not used to your kind . . . out here. Let's go have a drink."

That jarred upon Pan, but he followed as the girl led him and Brown to a table.

"Panhandle, are you going to stay here in Marco?" she inquired, leaning on her white round arms.

"Yes, if I find my folks," he replied simply. "They lost all they had . . . ranch, cattle, horses . . . and moved out here. I never knew until I went back home. Makes me feel pretty mean. But Dad was doing well when I left home."

"Mother . . . sister, too?"

"Yes. And my sister Alice must be quite a girl now," mused Pan.

"And you're going to help them?" she asked softly.

"I should smile," said Pan feelingly.

"Then you mustn't buy drinks for me . . . or run after me . . . as I was going to make you do."

Pan was at a loss for a reply. As he gazed at her, conscious of a subtle change, someone pushed him on the back and then fell on his neck.

"If heah ain't Panhandle," burst out a husky voice.

Pan got up as best he could, and pulled free from the fellow. The voice had prepared Pan for an old acquaintance, and, when he saw the lean red face and blue eyes, he knew them.

"Well, I'll be darned. Blinky Moran! You son-of-a-gun! Drinking . . . the same as when I saw you last."

"Aw, Pan, mebbe I was . . . but seein' you . . . old pard . . . it's like cold sweet water on my hot face."

"Blink, I'm sure glad to see you," replied Pan warmly. "What're you doing out here?"

Moran braced himself; it was evident that this meeting had roused him.

"Pan, meet my pard, heah," he began, indicating a stalwart young man in overalls and high boots. "Gus Hans, 'puncher of Montana."

Pan shook hands with the grinning cowboy.

"Pard, yo're shakin' the paw of Panhandle Smith," announced Moran in solemn emotion. "This heah's the boy, friends. You've heerd me rave many's the time. He was my pard, my bunkmate, my brother. We rode the Cimarron together an' the Arkansaw, an' he was the only straight 'puncher in the Long Bar C outfit, that was drove out of Wyomin'. His beat never forked a hoss or coiled a rope. An', pard, I'd been a rustler but fer Panhandle. More'n oncet he throwed his gun fer me, an'. . . ."

"Say, Blink, I'll have to choke you," interrupted Pan, laughing. "Now, you meet my friends here, Miss Louise . . . and Charley Brown."

Pan did not miss the effect the bright-eyed, red-lipped girl made upon the cowboys, especially Moran, who had always succumbed easily to feminine charms.

"Blinky, you've been drinking too much to dance," Louise remarked presently.

Then, rising from the table, she went around to Pan, and leaned up to him with both wistfulness and recklessness in her face.

"Panhandle Smith, I'll leave you to your friends," she said. "But don't you drift in here again . . . for if you do . . . I'll forget my sacrifices for little Alice. . . . There!"

She kissed him and ran off without a backward glance.

Blinky fell into a chair, overcome by some unusual emotion. He stared comically at Pan.

"Say, ole pard, you used to be shy of skirts!" he expostulated.

"Reckon I am yet, for all the evidence," Pan retorted, half amused and half angry at the girl.

Charley Brown joined in the mirth at Pan's expense.

"Guess the drinks are on me," he said. "And they'll be the last."

"Pan, that there girl is Louise Melliss!" ejaculated Moran.

"Is it? Well, who in the deuce is she?"

"Say, cowboy, quit your foolin'."

"Aw! Reckon I'm pretty much of a tenderfoot," returned Pan. His regret was for the pretty, audacious girl, whose boldness of approach he had not understood.

"Don't you come ridin' around heah fer thet little devil to get stuck on you," warned Moran. "She's shore a-goin' to give young Hardman a trimmin'. An' let her do it!"

"Oh! So you don't care much about young Hardman?" Pan inquired with interest. He certainly felt that he was falling into news.

"I'd like to throw a gun on him, an' oncet I mighty near done it," declared Moran.

"What for?"

"He an' another fellar jumped the only claim I ever struck that showed any color," went on the cowboy. "I went back one mawnin', an' there was Hardman an' a miner named Purcell. They ran me off, swore it was their claim. Purcell said he'd worked it before an' sold it to Jard Hardman. That's young Hardman's dad, an' he wouldn't fit in any square hole. I went to Matthews an' raised a holler. But I couldn't prove nothin'. An', Pan, thet claim is a mine now, payin' well."

"Tough luck, Blink. You always did have the darnedest luck. . . . Say, Brown, is that sort of deal worked often?"

"Common as dirt, in the early days of a strike," replied Brown. "I haven't heard of any claim jumpin' just lately, though. If a fellow leaves his claim for a day or a week, he's liable to come back an' find someone has jumped it. I never leave mine in the daytime, an' I have witnesses to that."

"Blinky, I came out here to find my dad," said Pan. "Have you ever run across him?"

"Nope. Never heerd of him. I'd shore have asked about you."

"How am I going to find out quick if Dad is here, and where?"

"Easy as pie. Go to the stage office, where they get the mail an' express. Matty Jones has been handlin' thet since this heah burg was a kid in short dresses."

"Good. I'll go the first thing in the morning. Now, you knock-kneed, bowlegged two-bit of a cowpuncher! What're you doing with those things on your boots?"

"Huh? What things?" queried Moran.

"Why, those long shiny things that jingle when you walk."

"Haw! Haw! Say, Pan, I might ask you the same. What you travel with them spurs on your boots fer?"

"I tried traveling without them, but I couldn't feel that I was moving."

"Wal, by gum, I been needin' mine. Ask Gus there. We've

been wranglin' wild hosses. Broomtails they calls them heah. We've been doin' pretty good. Hardman an' Wiggett pay twelve dollars an' four bits a hoss on the hoof. Right heah in Marco. We could get more if we could risk shippin' to Saint Louis. But thet't too tough of a job. Later, when we ketch a thousand haid, we may try it," Moran explained.

"A thousand head!"

"Shore. An' I'm just tellin' you, Pan, thet we can make it. But ketchin' these wild hosses in any number hasn't been done yet. Hardman has an outfit ridin'. But them fellars couldn't get away from their own dust. Suppose you throw in with us, Pan. You've chased wild hosses."

"Not such an awful lot, Blink. That game depends on the lay of the land."

"Shore. An' it lays bad in these parts. Will you throw in with us? An' have you got any money?"

"Yes to both questions, old-timer. But I've got to find Dad before I get careless with my money. Where are you boys staying?"

"We got a camp just out of town. We eat at the chink's when we're heah, an' thet's every few days. We got lots of room an' welcome for you, but no bedroll."

"I'll buy an outfit in the morning and throw it in with you. Hello, there's shooting. Gun play. Let's get out of this place where there's more room and air."

With that they, and many others, left the hall and joined in the moving crowd in the street. The night was delightfully cool. Stars shone white in a velvet sky. The dry wind from mountain and desert blew in their faces. Pan halted at the steps of the hotel.

"Blink, I'm going to turn in. Call for me in the morning. I can't tell you how glad I am that I ran into you boys. And you, too, Brown. I'd like to see more of you."

Pan was up bright and early, enjoying the keen desert air, and the vast difference between Marco at night and at dawn. The little spell of morbid doubt and worry that had settled upon him did not abide in the clear rosy light of day. Hope and thrill resurged in him.

Blinky and his partner soon appeared, and quarreled over which should carry Pan's luggage out to their quarters.

Pan decidedly preferred the locality to that he had just left. The boys had a big tent set up on a framework of wood, an open shed that they used as a kitchen, and a big corral. The site was up on a gradual slope, somewhat above the town, and rendered attractive by a small brook and straggling cedars. They had a Mexican cook who was known everywhere as Lying Juan.

The boys talked so fast they almost neglected to eat their breakfast. They were full of enthusiasm, which fact Pan could not but see was owing to his arrival. It amused him. Moran, like many other cowboys, had always attributed to Pan a prowess and character he felt sure were undeserved. Yet it touched him.

"Wal, old-timer, we'll rustle now," Moran finally said. "We've got about fifty broomies out heah in a cañon. We'll drive 'em in, an', also, some saddle horses for you."

"I'll buy a horse," interposed Pan.

"You'll do nothin' of the sort," Blinky declared stoutly. "Ain't we got a string of hosses? . . . an' there shore might be one of them good enough even for Panhandle Smith."

Gus came trotting up on a spirited sorrel, leading two other well-pointed horses, saddled, champing their bits. Sight of them was good for Pan's eyes. He would never long have been happy away from horses. Moran leaped astride one of them, and then said hesitatingly: "Pard, shore hope you hev good luck findin' your dad."

Pan watched them ride away down the slope to the road, and around a bend out of sight. It was wonderful country that faced him: cedar, piñon, and sage, colored hills and flats, walls of yellow rock stretched away, and dim purple mountains all around. If his keen eyes did not deceive him, there was a bunch of wild horses grazing on top of the first hill.

Pan shaved, put on a clean flannel shirt and a new scarf, and, leaving his coat behind, he strode off toward the town. The business of the day had begun, and there was considerable bustle. Certainly Marco showed no similarity to a cattle town. Somebody directed him to the stage and express office, a plain board building off the main street. Three men lounged before it, one on the steps, and the others against the hitching rail. Pan took them in before they paid any particular attention to him.

" 'Morning, gents," he said easily. "Is the agent, Jones, around?"

"Howdy, stranger," replied one of them. "Jones just stepped over to the bank. He'll be back *pronto*."

Another of the group straightened up to run a hard gray eye from Pan's spurs to his sombrero, and back for a second glance at his low-hanging gun. He was a tall man, in loose tan garments, trousers stuffed in his boots. He had a big sandy mustache. He moved to face Pan, and, either by accident or design, the flap of his coat fell back to expose a bright silver shield on his vest.

"Reckon you're new in these parts," he queried.

"Yep. Just rode in," replied Pan cheerfully.

"See you're packin' hardware," went on the other, with significant glance at Pan's gun.

Pan at once took this man to be Matthews, the town marshal mentioned by Charley Brown. He had not needed

Brown's hint; he had encountered many sheriffs of like stripe. Pan, usually the kindliest and most genial of cowboys, returned the marshal's curious scrutiny with a cool stare.

"Am I packing a gun?" Pan rejoined with pretended surprise, as he looked down at hip. "Sure, so I am. Clean forgot it, mister. Habit of mine."

"What's a habit?" snapped the other.

Pan knew he was going to have dealings with this man, and the sooner they began the better.

"Why, my packing a gun . . . when I'm in bad company," said Pan.

"Pretty strong talk, cowboy, west of the Rockies. I'm Matthews, the town marshal."

"I knew that, and I'm right glad to meet you," Pan responded pertly. He made no move to meet the half-proffered hand, and his steady gaze disconcerted the marshal.

Another man came briskly up, carrying papers in his hand.

"Are you the agent, Mister Jones?" asked Pan.

"I am thet air, young fellar."

"Can I see you a moment . . . on business?"

"Come right in." He ushered Pan into his office and shut the door.

"My name's Smith," began Pan hurriedly. "I'm hunting for my dad . . . Bill Smith. Do you know him . . . if he's in Marco?"

"Bill Smith's cowboy? Wal, put her thar," burst out the other heartily, shoving out a big hand. His surprise and pleasure were marked. "Know Bill? Wal, I should smile. We're neighbors an' good friends."

Pan was so overcome with relief and joy that he could not speak for a moment, but he wrung the agent's hand.

"Wal, now, sort of hit you in the gizzard, hey?" he queried with humor and sympathy. He released his hand and put it on

Pan's shoulder. "I've heard all about you, cowboy. Bill always talked a lot . . . until lately. Reckon he's deep hurt thet you never wrote."

"I've been pretty low-down," replied Pan with agitation. "But I never meant to be . . . I just drifted along. . . . Always I was going back home soon. But I didn't. And I haven't written home for two years."

"Wal, forget thet now, son," said the agent kindly. "You've been a wild one, if reports comin' to Bill was true. But you've come home to make up to him. Lord knows he needs you, boy."

"Yes . . . I'll make it . . . up," Pan replied, trying to swallow his emotion. "Tell me."

"Well, I wish I had better news to tell," replied Jones, gravely shaking his head. "Your dad's had tough luck. He lost his ranch in Texas, as I reckon you know, an' he follered . . . the man who'd done him out here to try to make him square up. Bill only got a worse deal. Then he got started again pretty good an' lost out because of a dry year. Now he's workin' in Carter's wagon shop. He's a first-rate carpenter. But his wages are small, an' he can't never get nowheres. He's talked some of wild hoss wranglin'. But thet takes an outfit, which he ain't got. I'll give you a hunch, son. If you can stake your dad to an outfit an' throw in with him, you might give him another start."

Pan had on his tongue an enthusiastic reply to that, but the entrance of the curious Matthews halted him.

"Thank you, Mister Jones," he said cagerly. "Where'll I find Carter's wagon shop?"

"Other end of town. Right down Main Street. You can't miss it."

Pan hurried out, and through the door he heard Matthews's loud voice. "Carter's wagon shop. . . . By thunder, I've got the hunch! That cowboy is Panhandle Smith!"

Pan smiled grimly to himself as he passed on out of hearing. The name and fame that had meant so little to him back on the prairie ranges might stand him in good stead out here west of the Rockies.

The way appeared long, and the line of stone houses and board shacks never-ending. At last he reached the outskirts of Marco, and espied the building and sign he was so eagerly seeking.

Pan entered the shop and espied a man wielding a hammer on a wheel. His back was turned. But Pan knew him. He approached leisurely. The moment seemed big, splendid.

"Howdy, Dad!" he called, at the end of one of the hammer strokes.

His father's lax figure stiffened. He dropped the wheel, then the hammer. But not on the instant did he turn. His posture was strained, doubtful. Then he sprang erect, and whirled.

"For the good . . . Lord's sake . . . if it ain't Pan!" he gasped. And to Pan's amaze he felt himself crushed in his father's arms. That sort of thing had never been Bill Smith's way. He thrilled to it, and tried again to beat back the remorse mounting higher. His father released him, and drew back. His working face smoothed out.

"Wal, Pan, you come back now . . . after long ago I gave up hopin'?" he queried haltingly.

"Yes, Dad," Pan began with swift rush of words. "I'm sorry. I always meant to come home. But one thing and another prevented. I never heard of your troubles. I never knew you needed me. You didn't write. Why didn't you tell me? But forget that. I rode the ranges . . . drifted with the cowboys . . . till I got homesick. Now I've found you . . . and, well,

I want to make up to you and Mother."

"A-huh! Sounds like music to me," Bill Smith replied, growing slow and cool. He eyed Pan up and down, walked around him twice. Then he suddenly burst out: "Wal, you long-legged, strappin' son-of-a-gun! If sight of you ain't good for sore eyes! A-huh! Look where he packs that gun!"

With slow strange motion he reached down to draw Pan's gun from its holster. Pan realized what his father knew, what he thought. The moment was sickening.

"Pan, I've kept tab on you for years," spoke his father slowly. "But I'd have heard, even if I hadn't took pains to learn. Panhandle Smith! You hard-ridin', gun-throwin' son of mine! Once my heart broke because you drifted with the wild cowpunchers . . . but now . . . I believe I'm glad!"

"Dad, never mind range talk. You know how cowboys brag and blow. I'm not ashamed to face you and Mother. I've come clean, Dad."

"But, Son, you've . . . you've used that gun," Bill Smith whispered hoarsely.

"Sure I have. On some two-legged coyotes an' skunks. And maybe greasers, I forget."

"Panhandle Smith!" ejaculated his father, refusing to take the matter in Pan's light vein. "They know here in Marco. You're known, Pan, here west of the Rockies."

"Well, what of it?" flashed Pan. "I should think you'd be glad. Reckon it was all good practice for what I'll have to do out here."

"Don't talk that way. You've read my mind," Smith replied huskily. "I'm almost sorry you came. Yet, right now, I feel more of a man than for years."

"Dad, you can tell me everything some other time," rejoined Pan, throwing off that sinister spell. "Now I only want to know about Mother and Alice."

"They're well an' fine, Son, though your mother grieves for you. An' Alice, she's a big girl, goin' to school an' helpin' with the work. An', Pan, you've got a baby brother nearly two years old."

"Jumping cowbells!" shouted Pan in delight. "Where are they? Tell me quick."

"We live on a farm a mile or so out. I rent it for almost nothin'. I've got an option on it, an' it shore is a bargain. You'll. . . ."

"Stop talking about it. I'll buy the farm," interrupted Pan. "But where is it?"

"Keep right on this road. Second farmhouse," said his father, pointing to the west. "I'd go with you, but I promised some work. But I'll be at home at noon. Hey, hold on. There's more to tell. You'll get a . . . a jolt. Wait."

But Pan rushed out of the shop, and took to the road with the stride of a giant.

At last Pan reached the wagon gate that led into the farm. It bordered an orchard of fair-sized trees. He cut across the orchard so as to reach the house more quickly. It was still almost hidden among the trees. Smell of hay, of fruit, of the barnyard assailed his nostrils. His heart swelled full high in his breast.

Suddenly he espied a woman through the trees. She was quite close. He almost ran. No, it could not be his mother. This was a girl, lithe, tall, swift-stepping. His mother had been rather short and stout. Could this girl be his sister Alice? The swift supposition was absurd, because Alice was only about ten. He hurried around some trees to intercept her.

Suddenly he came out of the shade to confront her, face to face, in the open sunlight. She uttered a cry and dropped something she had been carrying.

"Pan! Pan!" she cried, and moved toward him, her eyes widening, shining with a light he had never seen in another woman's.

"Pan! Don't you . . . know me?"

"Sure . . . but I don't know who you are," Pan muttered in bewilderment.

"I'm Lucy! Oh, Pan . . . you've come back," she burst out huskily, with a deep break in her voice.

She seemed to leap toward him—in the arms he flung wide as, with tremendous shock, he recognized her name, her voice, her eyes. It was a moment beyond reason. . . . He was crushing her to his breast, kissing her in a frenzy of sudden realization of love. Lucy! Lucy! Little Lucy Blake, his baby, his child sweetheart, his schoolmate! And the hunger of the long lonely years, never realized, leaped to his lips now.

He was shaken to his depths by the revelation that now came to him. He had always loved Lucy! Never anyone else, never knowing until this precious moment! What a glorious trick for life to play him. He held her, wrapped her closer, bent his face to her fragrant hair. It was dull gold now. He kissed it, conscious of unutterable gratitude and exaltation.

She stirred, put her hands to his breast, and broke away from him, tragic-eyed, strange.

"Pan, I . . . I was beside myself," she whispered. "Forgive me. . . . Oh, the joy of seeing you. It was too much. Go to your mother. She . . . will. . . ."

"Yes, presently, but, Lucy, you're so changed . . . so . . . so . . . Lucy, you're beautiful. I've come back to you. I always loved you. I didn't know it as I do now, but I've been true to you. Lucy, I swear. And I've come back to love you, to make up for absence, to take care of you . . . marry you. Oh, darling, I know you've waited for me."

Rapture and agony seemed to be struggling for the mastery over Lucy. Pan suddenly divined that this was the meaning of her emotion.

"Don't you know?" she whispered finally, warding him off. "Haven't you heard?"

"Nothing," Pan replied hoarsely, fighting an icy fear. "What's wrong?"

She made no reply, except to cover her face with shaking hands.

"Lucy, you must love me," he rushed on almost incoherently. "You gave yourself away. It lifted me . . . changed me. All my life I've loved you, though I never realized it. . . . Your kisses . . . they made me know myself. . . . But say that you love me!"

"Yes, Pan, I do love you," she replied quietly, lifting her eyes to his.

"Then nothing else matters!" cried Pan. "Whatever's wrong, I'll make it right. Don't forget that. I've much to make up for. Forgive me for this . . . this . . . whatever has hurt you so. I'll go now to Mother and see you later. You'll stay?"

"I live here with your people," Lucy replied, and walked away through the trees.

Flowers that he recognized as the favorites of his mother bordered the sandy path around the cabin. The house had been constructed of logs and later improved with a frame addition, unpainted, weather-stained, covered with vines. A cozy little porch, with wide eaves and a windbreak of vines, faced the south. He heard a child singing, then a woman's mellow voice.

Pan drew a long breath and took off his sombrero. It had come—the moment he had long dreamed of. He stepped loudly upon the porch.

"Who's there?" called the voice. It made Pan's heart beat fast. In deep husky tones he replied: "Just a poor starved cowboy, ma'am, beggin' a little grub."

"Gracious me!" the speaker exclaimed, and her footsteps thudded on the floor inside.

Pan knew his words would fetch her. Then he saw her come to the door. Years, trouble, pain had wrought their havoc, but he would have known her at first sight among a thousand women.

"Mother!" he called poignantly, and stepped toward her with his arms out.

She seemed stricken. The kindly eyes changed, rolled. She gasped and fainted in his arms.

A little later, when she had recovered from the shock and the rapture of Pan's return, they sat in the neat little room.

"Bobby, don't you know your big brother?" Pan was repeating to the big-eyed boy who regarded him so solemnly. Bobby was fascinated by this stranger.

"Mother, I reckon you'll never let Bobby be a cowboy," teased Pan.

"Never," she murmured fervently.

"Well, he might do worse," went on Pan thoughtfully. "But we'll make a plain rancher out of him, with a leaning to horses. How's that?"

"I'd like it, but not in a wild country like this," she replied.

"Reckon we'd do well to figure on a permanent home in Arizona, where both summers and winters are pleasant. I've heard a lot about Arizona. It's a land of wonderful grass and ranges, fine forests, cañons. We'll go there, someday."

"Then, Pan, you've come home to stay?" she asked with agitation.

"Yes, Mother," he assured her, squeezing the worn hand that kept reaching to touch him. "There's a million things to talk about. You say Alice is in school. When will she be home?"

"At noon, Pan," she went on hesitatingly. "Lucy Blake lives with us now."

"Yes, I met Lucy outside," replied Pan, drawing a deep breath. "But first about Dad. Is he well in health?"

"He's well enough. Really he does two men's work. Worry drags him down."

"We'll cheer him up. At Littletown I heard a little about Dad's bad luck. Now you tell me everything."

"There's little to tell, Pan," she replied sadly. "Your father made foolish deals back in Texas, the last and biggest part of which was with Jard Hardman. There came a bad year . . . *año seco,* the Mexicans call it. Failure of crops left your father ruined. He lost the farm. He found later that Hardman had cheated him out of his cattle. We followed Hardman out here. Our neighbors, the Blakes, had come ahead of us. Hardman not only wouldn't be square about the cattle deal, but he knocked your father out again, just as he had another start. In my mind it was worse than the cattle deal.

"We bought a homestead from a man named Sprague. This homestead had water, good soil, some timber and an undeveloped mining claim that turned out well. Then along comes Jard Hardman with claims, papers, witnesses, and law back of him. He claimed to have gotten possession of the homestead from the original owner. It was all a lie. But they put us off. Then your father tried several things that did not pan out. Now we're here . . . and he has to work in the wagon shop to pay the rent."

"A-huh!" replied Pan, relieving his oppressed breast with an effort. "And now about Lucy. How does it come she's living with you?"

"She had no home, poor girl," his mother responded hastily. "She came out here with her father and uncle. Her mother died soon after you left us. Jem Blake had interests with Hardman back in Texas. He talked big . . . and drank a good deal. He and Hardman quarreled. It was the same big deal that ruined your father. But Jem came to New Mexico with Hardman. They were getting along all right when we arrived. But trouble soon arose . . . and that over Lucy. Young Dick Hardman . . . you certainly ought to remember him, Pan . . . fell madly in love with Lucy. Dick was always a wild boy. Here in Marco he went the pace.

"Well, bad as Jard Hardman is, he loves that boy and would move heaven and earth for him. Lucy despised Dick. The more he ran after her, the more she despised him. The more she flouted Dick, the wilder he drank and gambled. Now here comes the painful part of it. Jem Blake went utterly to the bad, so your father says, though Lucy believes she can save him. I do, too. Jem was only weak. Jard Hardman ruined him.

"Finally Dick enlisted his father in his cause, and they forced Jem to try to make Lucy marry Dick. She refused. She left her father's place and went to live with her Uncle Bill, who was an honest fine man. But he was shot in the Yellow Mine. By accident, they gave out, but your father scouts that idea. . . . Oh, those dreadful gambling hells! Life is cheap here. Lucy came to live with us. She taught school. But she had to give that up. Dick Hardman and other wild young fellows made her life wretched. Besides, she was never safe. We persuaded her to give it up. And then the . . . the worst happened." Mrs. Smith paused and lifted an appealing hand to Pan.

"What . . . what was it, Mother?"

"They put Jem in jail," she began.

"What for?"

"To hold him there, pending action back in Texas. Jem Blake was a cattle thief. There's little doubt of that, your fa-

61

ther says. You know there's law back East, at least now in some districts. Well, Jard Hardman is holding Jem in jail. It seems Hardman will waive trial, provided . . . provided. . . . Oh, how can I tell you?"

"Oh, I see!" cried Pan, leaping in fierce passion. "They will try to force Lucy to marry Dick to save her father."

"Yes. That's it. And Pan, my son . . . she has consented."

"So that was what made her act so strange. Poor Lucy! Dick Hardman was a skunk when he was a kid. Now he's a skunk-bitten coyote. . . ."

"Pan, what can you do?"

"Lucy hasn't married him yet? Tell me quick," Pan asked suddenly.

"Oh, no. She has only promised. She doesn't trust those men. She wants papers signed to clear her father. They laugh at her. But Lucy is no fool. When she sacrifices herself, it'll not be for nothing."

Pan slowly sank down on the big blue gun with which Bobby was playing. It fascinated Pan. Sight of it brought the strange cold sensation that seemed like a wind through his being.

"Mother, how old is Lucy?" he asked, forcing himself to be calm.

"She's nearly seventeen, but looks older."

"Not of age yet. Yes, she looks twenty. She's a woman, Mother."

"What did Lucy do and say when she saw you?" asked his mother.

"She ran right into my arms. We just met, Mother, and the old love leaped."

"Mercy, what a terrible situation for you both, especially for Lucy. Pan, what can you do?"

"Mother, I don't know, I can't think. It's too sudden. I'll

never let her marry Dick Hardman. But how to save Jem Blake?"

"Pan, do you think it can be done?"

"My dear Mother, I know it. Only I can't think now. I'm new here. And handicapped by concern for you, for Lucy, for Dad. Lord, if I was back in the Cimarron . . . it'd be easy!"

"Only save her father, Pan, and you will be blessed with such woman's love as you never dreamed of. It may be hard, though, for you to change her mind."

"I won't try, Mother."

"Go to her, then, and fill her with the hope you've given me."

Chapter Seven

From a thick clump of trees Pan had watched Lucy, spied upon her with only love, tenderness, pity in his heart. But he did not know her. It seemed incredible that he could confess to himself he loved her. Had the love he had cherished as a child suddenly, as if by magic, leaped into love for a woman? What then was this storm within him, this outward bodily trembling from the tumult within?

As she paced away from him the small gold head, the heavy braid of her hair, the fine build of her, not robust, yet strong and full, answered then and there the wondering query of his admiration. Then she turned to pace back. She had been weeping, yet her face was white. Indeed, she did not look older than her seventeen years. Closer she came. Then Pan's gaze got as far as her eyes and fixed there. Unmasked now, true to the strife of her soul, they betrayed to Pan the thing he yearned so to know. Not only her love but her revolt.

That was enough for him. In a few seconds his feelings underwent a tremendous gamut of change, at last to set with the certainty of a man's love for his one woman. This conviction seemed consciously backed by the stern fact of his cool reckless spirit. He was what the range of that period had made him.

He stepped out to confront Lucy, smiling and cool.

"Howdy, Lucy," he drawled, with the cowboy sang-froid she must know well.

"Oh!" she cried, startled, and drawing back. Then she recovered.

"Let's sit down on the seat there, and get acquainted."

He put her in the corner of the bench so she would have to face him, and he began to talk as if there were no black trouble between them. He wanted her to know the story of his life from the time she had seen him last. He had two reasons for this: first to bridge that gap in their acquaintance, and secondly to let her know what the range had made him. It took him two hours in the telling, surely the sweetest hours he had ever spent, for he watched her warm to intense interest, forget herself, live over with him the lonely days and nights on the range, and glow radiant at his adventures, and pale and trembling over those bloody encounters that were as much a part of his experience as any others.

"That's my story, Lucy," he said in conclusion. "I'd have come back to you and home long ago if I'd known. But I was always broke. Then there was the talk about me. Panhandle Smith! So the years sped by. It's over now, and I've found you and my people all well. Nothing else matters to me. And your trouble and Dad's bad luck do not scare me. . . . Now tell me your story."

With simple directions she related the downfall of her father and how the disgrace and heartbreak had killed her mother. When she finished her story, she was crying.

"Lucy, don't cry. Just think . . . here we are!" he exclaimed as she ended.

"That's what . . . makes me cry."

"Very well. Here. Cry on my shoulder," he said. He held her, feeling the strain of her muscles slowly relax.

"Pan, this is . . . is foolish," she said, presently stirring. "I mean my crying here in your arms, as if it were a refuge. But, ah! I . . . I have needed someone . . . something so terribly."

"I don't see where it's foolish. Reckon it's very sweet and wonderful for me."

"Is it happiness for you . . . knowing it's wrong . . . and can never be again?" she whispered.

"Pure heaven!" he said. "Lucy, don't say this is wrong. You belong to me."

"My soul does, yes," she returned dreamily. And then, as if reminded of her bodily weakness, she moved away from him to the corner of the bench.

"All right, Lucy. Have it your way now. But you'll only have all the more to make up to me later," Pan said with resigned good nature.

"Pan, you don't seem to recognize anything but your own will," she returned ponderingly. "I've got to save my father. . . . There's only one way."

"Don't talk such rot to me," he flashed sharply. "You've been frightened into a deal that is terrible for you. No wonder. But you're only a kid yet. What do you know of men? These Hardmans are crooked. Matthews, he's crooked, too. Why, Lucy, I'm amazed that some miner or cowboy or gunfighter hasn't stopped them long ago."

"Pan, you must be wrong," she declared earnestly. "Hardman cheated Dad, yes. But that was only Dad's fault. His blindness in business. Hardman is a power here. And Matthews, too. You talk like a . . . a wild cowboy."

"Sure," replied Pan with a grim laugh. "And it'll take just a wild cowboy to clean up this mess. I'll go to see your father. And I'll call on Hardman. I'll talk sense and reason and business to these men. I know it'll not amount to beans, but I'll do it just to show you I can be deliberate and sane."

"Thank you . . . you frightened me so," she murmured.

"Pan, there was something terrible about you . . . then."

"Listen, Lucy," he began more seriously. "I've been here in Marco only a few hours. But this country is no place for us to settle down to live. I'm going to take you all down to Arizona. Dad and Mother will love the idea. I'll get your father out of jail. . . ."

"Pan, are you dreaming?" she interrupted in distress. "Dad is a rustler. He admits it. Back in Texas he can be jailed for years. All Hardman has to do is to send for officers to come take Dad. And I've got to marry Dick Hardman to save him."

"You poor little girl. Now, Lucy, let me tell you something. It's gospel truth, I swear. Rustler you call your dad. What's that? It means a cowman who had appropriated cattle not his own. He has driven off unbranded stock and branded it. There's no difference. Lucy, my dad rustled cattle. So have all the ranchers I ever rode for."

"What are you saying?" she gasped.

"I'm trying to tell you one of the queer facts about the ranges," replied Pan. "I've known cowmen to shoot rustlers. Cowmen who had themselves branded cattle not their own. This was a practice. They didn't think it crooked. They all did it. But it was crooked, when you come down to truth. And though that may not be legally as criminal as the stealing of branded cattle, to my mind it is just as bad. Your father began that way, Hardman caught him, and perhaps forced him into worse practice."

"Pan, are you trying to give me some hope?"

"Reckon I am. Things are not so bad. My Lord, suppose I'd been a month later!"

Lucy shook her head despondently. "It's worse now for me than if you had come. . . ."

"Why?" interrupted Pan.

67

"Because to see you . . . be with you like this . . . before I'm
. . . if I have to be married . . . is perfectly terrible. Afterward,
when it would be too late and I had lost something . . . self-
respect or more, then I might not care."

The hot blood rushed to Pan's face. He struggled to control himself.

"Lucy! Haven't I told you that you're not going to marry
Dick Hardman?" he burst out.

"I must save Dad. You might indeed get him out of jail
some way. But that would not save him."

"Certainly it would," Pan rejoined curtly. "In another
state he would be perfectly safe."

"They'll trail him anywhere. No, that won't do. We
haven't time. Dick is pressing me hard to marry him at once,
or his father will prosecute Dad. I promised. And today . . .
this morning . . . Dick is coming here to get me to set the
day."

"What kind of woman are you?" asked Pan hoarsely. "If
you love me, it's a crime to marry him. Women do these
things, I know . . . sell themselves. But they kill their souls.
If you could save your father from being hanged, it would
still be wrong. You must care for this skunk Dick Hardman."

"Care for him?" she cried, shamefaced and furious. "I
hate him!"

"Then, if you marry him, you'll be crooked. To yourself.
To me."

"I will . . . I must. . . ."

"Lucy!" he thundered. "Say you love me!"

"I . . . I love you," she said, the scarlet blood mounting to
her pale face.

"How do you love me?" he queried relentlessly, with his
heart mounting high.

"Always I've loved you . . . since I was a baby."

"As a brother?"

"Yes."

"But we're man and woman now. This is my one chance for happiness. I don't want you . . . I wouldn't have you unless you love me as I do you. Be honest with me. Do you love me as I do you?"

"Heaven help me . . . yes," she replied almost inaudibly. For the moment, at least, love conquered her.

Pan was wrenched out of the ecstasy of that moment by the pound of hoofs and the crashing of brush. He could not disengage himself from Lucy's arms before a horse and rider were upon them. Nevertheless, Pan recognized the intruder.

Dick Hardman showed the most abject astonishment. He stared from Lucy to Pan and back again. Black fury suddenly possessed him.

"You . . . you . . . !" he yelled stridently, moving to dismount.

"Stay on your horse," commanded Pan.

"Who are you?" bellowed Hardman.

"Howdy, Skunk Hardman," rejoined Pan with cool impudence. "Reckon you ought to know me."

"Pan Smith," gasped the other hoarsely, and he turned lividly white. "I knew you last night. But I couldn't place you."

"Well, Mister Dick Hardman, I knew you the instant I set eyes on you . . . sitting there gambling . . . with the pretty bare-armed girl on your chair," returned Pan.

"Of all the nerve! You . . . you damned cowpuncher," raved Hardman in a fury. "Now you make tracks out of here or I'll . . . I'll . . . it'll be the worse fer you, Pan Smith. . . . Lucy Blake is as good as married to me."

"Nope, you're wrong, Dick," Pan snapped insolently.

"I've got here just in time to save her from that doubtful honor."

"You'd break your engagement to me?" Hardman rasped huskily, and he actually shook in his saddle.

"I have broken it."

"Lucy, tell me he lies!" begged Hardman, turning to her in poignant distress. If he had any good in him, it showed then.

Lucy came out from the shade of the tree into the sunlight. She was pale, but composed.

"Dick, it's true," she said steadily. "I've broken my word. I can't marry you . . . I love Pan. It would be a sin to marry you now."

Hardman's face grew frightful to see—beastly with rage. "I'll fix you, Lucy Blake. And I'll put your cow-thief father behind the bars for life."

Pan leaped at Hardman, and struck him a body blow that sent him tumbling out of his saddle to thud on the ground. The frightened horse ran down the path.

"You dirty-mouthed cur," said Pan. "Get up and, if you've got a gun . . . throw it."

Hardman laboriously got to his feet. The breath had been partly knocked out of him. Baleful eyes rolled at Pan. Instinctive wrath, however, had been given a backset. Hardman had been forced to think of something besides the frustration of his imperious will.

"I'm . . . not . . . packing . . . my gun," he panted heavily. "You saw . . . that . . . Pan Smith."

"Well, you'd better pack it after this," replied Pan with contempt. "Because I'm liable to throw on you at sight."

"I'll have . . . you run . . . out of this country," Dick replied huskily.

"Bah! Don't waste your breath. Run me out of this country? You and your crooked father and your two-bit of a

70

sheriff partner would do well to leave this country. Savvy that? Now get out of here *pronto*."

Hardman gave Pan a ghastly stare and wheeled away to stride down the path. Once he turned to flash his convulsed face at Lucy. Then he passed out of sight among the trees.

Pan stood gazing down the green aisle. He had acted true to himself. How impossible to meet this situation in any other way. It meant the spilling of blood. He knew it—accepted it—and made no attempt to change the cold passion deep within him. Lucy and his mother and father would suffer. But would they not suffer more if he did not confront this conflict as his hard training dictated? He was almost afraid to turn and look at Lucy. Just a little while before he had promised her forbearance. So his amaze was great when she faced him, violet eyes ablaze, to clasp him, and creep close to him.

"Panhandle Smith!" she whispered, gazing up into his face. "I heard your story. It thrilled me. But I never understood . . . till you faced Dick Hardman. Oh, what have you done to me? Oh, Pan, you have saved me from ruin."

Chapter Eight

Pan and Lucy did not realize the passing of time until they were called to dinner. As they stepped upon the little porch, Lucy tried to withdraw her hand from Pan's, but did not succeed.

"See here," he said very seriously, yielding to an urge he could not resist. "Wouldn't it be wise for us to . . . to get married at once?"

Lucy blushed furiously. "Pan! Are you crazy?"

"Reckon I am," he replied ruefully. "But I got to thinking how I'll be out after wild horses. . . . And I'm afraid that something might happen. Please marry me this afternoon."

"Pan! You're terrible," cried Lucy, and, snatching away her hand, scarlet of face she rushed into the house ahead of him.

He followed, to find Lucy gone. His father was smiling, and his mother had wide-open, hopeful eyes. A slim young girl, with freckles, grave sweet eyes, and curly hair was standing by a window. She turned and devoured him with those shy eyes. From that look he knew who this was.

"Alice! Little sister!" he exclaimed. "Well, by golly, this is great."

It did not take long for Pan to grasp that a subtle change had come over his mother and father. Not the excitement of his presence or the wonder about Lucy accounted for it, but a difference, a lessening of strain, a relief. Pan sensed a reliance upon him that they were not yet conscious of.

"Son, what was the matter with Lucy?" his father inquired shrewdly.

"Why, nothing to speak of," Pan replied nonchalantly. "Reckon she was a little flustered because I wanted her to marry me this afternoon."

"Good gracious!" cried his mother. "You are a cowboy. Lucy marry you when she's engaged to another man!"

"Mother, that's broken off. Don't remind me of it. I want to look pleasant, so you'll all be glad I'm home."

"Glad!" His mother laughed with a catch in her voice. "My prayers have been answered. Come now to dinner."

They went into the little whitewashed kitchen, where Pan had to stoop to avoid the ceiling, and took seats at the table. Pan feasted his eyes. His mother had not forgotten the things that he had always liked. Alice acted as waitress, and Bobby sat in a highchair, beaming upon Pan. At that juncture Lucy came in. She had changed her gray blouse to one of white, with wide collar that was cut a little low and showed the golden contour of her superb neck. She had put up her hair. Pan could not take his eyes off her. In hers, he saw a dancing subdued light, and a beautiful rose color in her cheeks.

"Well, I've got to eat," said Pan, as if by way of explanation and excuse for removing his gaze from this radiant creature.

Thus his homecoming proved to be a happier event than he had ever dared to hope for.

"Dad, let's go out and have a talk," proposed Pan after dinner.

As they walked down toward the corrals, Pan's father was silent, yet it was clear he labored with suppressed feeling.

"All right, fire away," he burst out at last, "but first tell me, for heaven's sake, how'd you do it?"

"What?" queried Pan.

"Mother! She's *well*. She wasn't well at all," exclaimed the older man, breathing hard. "An' that girl! Did you ever see such eyes?"

"Reckon I never did," replied Pan with joyous bluntness.

"This mornin' I left Lucy crushed. Her eyes were like lead. An' now! Pan, I'm thankin' God for them. But tell me how'd you do it?"

"Dad, I don't know women very well, but I reckon they live by their hearts. You can bet that happiness for them means a lot to me. I felt pretty low-down. That's gone. I could crow like Bobby. Dad, I've a big job on my hands, but I think I'm equal to it. Are you going to oppose me?"

"No!" spat his father, losing his pipe in his vehemence. "Son, I lost my cattle, my ranch. An' then my nerve. I'm not makin' excuses. I just fell down. But I'm not too old to make another start with you to steer me."

"Good," replied Pan. "Then let's get right down to straight poker."

"Play your game, Pan."

"First off, then . . . we don't want to settle in this country."

"Pan, you've called me right on the first hand," declared his father, cracking his fist on the corral gate. "I know this's no country for the Smiths. But I followed Jard Hardman here, I hoped to. . . ."

"Never mind explanations, Dad," interrupted Pan. "We're looking to the future. We won't settle here. We'll go on to Arizona. I had a pard who came from Arizona. All day long and half the night that bronco buster would rave about Arizona. Well, he won me over. Arizona must be wonderful."

"But, Pan, isn't it desert country?"

"Arizona is every kind of country," Pan replied earnestly. "It's a big territory, Dad. Pretty wild yet, too, but not like these mining claim countries, with the Yellow Mines. Arizona is getting settlers in the valleys where there's water and grass. Lots of fine pine timber that will be valuable someday. I know just where we'll strike for. If it suits you, the thing is settled. We go to Arizona."

"Fine, Pan," said his father. "*When* will we go?"

"That's to decide," Pan answered thoughtfully. "I've got some money. Not much. But we could get there and start on it. I believe, though, that we'd do better to stay here . . . this fall anyway . . . and round up a bunch of these wild horses. Five hundred horses, a thousand, at twelve dollars a head . . . why, Dad, it would start us in a big way."

"Son, I should smile it would," returned Bill Smith with fiery enthusiasm. "But can you do it?"

"Dad, if these broomies are as thick as I hear they are, I sure can make a stake. Last night I fell in with two cowboys, Blinky Moran and Gus Hans. They're chasing wild horses, and want me to throw in with them. Now, with you and maybe a couple more riders, we can make a big drive. If these broomtails are thick here . . . well, I don't want to set your hopes too high. But wait until I show you."

"Pan, there's ten thousand wild horses in that one valley across the mountain there. Hot Springs Valley, they call it."

"Then, by George, we've got to take the risk," declared Pan decisively.

"Risk of what?"

"Trouble with that Hardman outfit. It can't be avoided. I'd have to bluff them out or fight them down, right off. Dick is a yellow skunk. Jard Hardman is a bad man in any pinch. But not on an even break. I don't mean that. If that were all. But he's treacherous. And his henchman, this two-bit of a sheriff, he's no man to face you on the square. I'll swear he can be bluffed.

"Jard Hardman will be the hard nut to crack. Now, Dad, back in Littletown I learned what he did to you. And Lucy's story gave me another angle on that. It's pretty hard to overlook. I'm not swearing I can do so. But I'd like to know how you feel about it."

"Son, I'd be scared to tell you," replied Smith in a husky voice, dropping his head.

"You needn't, Dad. We'll stay here till we catch and sell a bunch of horses," Pan said curtly. "Can you quit your job at the wagon shop?"

"Any time . . . an' won't I be glad to do it," returned Smith fervently.

"Well, you just quit, then," Pan remarked dryly. "So much is settled. Dad, I've got to get Jem Blake out of that jail."

"I reckoned so. It might be a job an' then again it mightn't. Depends on Jem. An' between you an' me, Pan, I've no confidence in Jem."

"That doesn't make any difference. I've got to get him out and send him away. Head him for Arizona, where we're going. . . . Is it a real jail?"

" 'Dobe mud an' stones," replied his father. "An Indian or a real man could break out of there any night. There are three guards, who change off every eight hours. One of them is a tough customer. Name's Hill. He used to be an outlaw. The other two are lazy loafers 'round town."

"All right, Dad," Pan said with cheerful finality. "Let's go back to the house and talk Arizona to Lucy and Mother for a little. Then I'll rustle along toward town. Tomorrow you come over to the boys' camp. It's on the other side of town, in a cedar flat, up that slope. We've got horses to try out and saddles to buy."

Chapter Nine

As Pan strode back along the road toward Marco, the whole world seemed to have changed.

He felt now for the first time in his life he had a mighty incentive, something tremendous and calling, to bring out that spirit of fire common to the daredevils of the range. He had touched only the last fringe of cowboy régime. Dodge and Abilene, the old Chisholm Trail, the hard-drinking, hardshooting days of an earlier Cimarron had gone. Life then had been but a chance of a card, the wink of an eye, the flip of a quirt. But Pan had ridden and slept with men who had seen those days. He had absorbed from them, and to him had come a later period, not comparable in any sense, yet rough, free, untamed, and still bloody.

He knew how to play his cards against such men as these. The more boldly he faced them, the more menacingly he went out of his way to meet them, the greater would be his advantage. If Matthews were another Hickok, the situation would have been vastly different. If there were any real fighting men on Hardman's side, Pan would recognize them in a single glance. He was an unknown quantity to them, that most irritating of newcomers to a wild place, the man with a name preceding him.

Pan came abreast of the building that he was seeking. It was part stone and part adobe, heavily and crudely built, with no windows on the side facing him. Approaching it, and turning the corner, he saw a wide-arched door leading into a small stone-floored room. He heard voices. In a couple of long strides Pan crossed the flat threshold. Two men were playing cards with a greasy deck. The one whose back was turned to Pan did not see him, but the other man jerked up from his bench, then sagged back with a strangely altering expression. He was young, dark, coarse, and he had a bullet hole in his chin.

Pan's recognition did not lag behind the other's. This was Handy MacNew, late of Montana, a cowboy who had drifted beyond the pale. He was one of that innumerable band that Pan had helped in some way or other. Handy had become a suspected murderer in the year following Pan's acquaintance with him.

"Howdy, men," Pan greeted them, giving no sign that he had recognized MacNew. "Which one of you is on guard here?"

"Me," MacNew replied, choking over the word. Slowly he got to his feet.

"You've got a prisoner in there named Blake," went on Pan. "I once lived near him. Will you let me talk to him?"

"Why, shore, stranger," MacNew responded with nervous haste, and, producing a key, he inserted it in the lock of a heavy whitewashed door.

Pan found himself ushered into a large room with small iron-barred windows on the west side. His experience of frontier jails had been limited, but those he had seen had been bare, empty, squalid cells. This, however, was evidently a luxurious kind of prison house. There were Indian blankets and rugs on the floor, an open fireplace with cheerful blaze, a table littered with books and papers, a washstand, a comfortable bed upon which reclined a man smoking and reading.

"Somebody to see you, Blake," called the guard, and he went out.

Blake sat up. As he did so, Pan's keen eye espied a bottle on the floor.

Pan approached leisurely, his swift thoughts revolving around a situation that looked peculiar to him. Blake was very much better cared for than could have been expected. Why?

"Howdy, Blake. Do you remember me?" asked Pan.

He did not in the least remember Lucy's father in this heavy blond man, lax of body and sodden of face.

"Somethin' familiar aboot you," replied Blake, studying Pan intently. "But I reckon you've got the best of me."

"Pan Smith," Pan said shortly.

"Wal!" Blake ejaculated as if shocked into memory, and slowly he rose to hold out a shaking hand. "Bill's kid . . . the little boy who stuck by my wife . . . when Lucy was born."

"Same boy, and he's sorry to find you in this fix," responded Pan forcefully. "And he's here to get you out."

Blake's face changed like that of a man suddenly stabbed. And he dropped his head. Manifestly the good in him had not been wholly killed by evil.

"Mister Blake, I've been to see Lucy," went on Pan, and swiftly he talked of the girl, her unhappiness, and the faith she still held in her father. "I've come to get you out of here, for Lucy's sake. We're all going to Arizona. You and Dad can make a new start in life."

"Oh, if I only could," groaned the man.

Pan reached out with quick hand and shook him. "Listen," he said low and eagerly. "How long is this guard MacNew on duty?"

"MacNew? The fellow outside is called Hurd. He's on till midnight."

"All right, my mistake," Pan went quickly. "I'll be here tonight about eleven. I'll have a horse for you, blanket, grub, gun, and money. I'll hold up this guard Hurd . . . get you out some way or other. You're to ride away. Take the road south. There are other mining camps. You'll not be followed. Make for Siccane, Arizona."

"Siccane, Arizona," echoed Blake, as a man in a dream of freedom.

"Yes, Siccane. Don't forget it. Stay there till we all come."

Pan straightened up, with deep expulsion of breath and tingling nerves. He had reached Blake. Whatever his doubts of the man, and they had been many, Pan divined that he could stir him, rouse him out of the lethargy of sordid indifference and forgetfulness. He would free him from this jail, and the shackles of Hardman in any case, but to find that it was possible to influence him gladdened Pan's heart. What would this not mean to Lucy.

The door opened behind Pan.

"Well, stranger, reckon yore time's up," called the jailer.

Pan gave the stunned Blake a meaningful look, and then without a word he left the room. The guard closed and locked the door. He looked up, with cunning, yet not wholly without pleasure. His companion at the card game had gone.

"Panhandle Smith," whispered the guard, half stretching out his hand, then withdrawing it.

"Shake, Mac," Pan said in a low voice. "It's a small world."

"It shore is," replied MacNew with an oath, wringing Pan's hand. "I'm known here as Hurd."

"A-huh. Well, Hurd, I'm not a talking man. But I want to remind you that you owe me a good turn."

"I savvy, Panhandle Smith," Hurd said with gleaming eyes, and he crooked a stubby thumb toward the door of Blake's jail.

"All right, cowboy," returned Pan with a meaningful

smile. "I'll drop around tonight about eleven."

Pan slowed up in his stride when he reached the business section of the town, and strolled along as if he were looking for someone. He was. He meant to have eyes in the back of his head henceforth. But he did not meet anyone he knew or see anyone who glanced twice at him.

He went into Black's General Merchandise Store to buy a saddle, a carbine, and a saddle sheath for it. Thus burdened, he walked out to the camp.

"Wal, if heah ain't ole Pan Smith," Blinky announced vociferously. "Gus, take a peep at him. I'll bet he's got hold of a grand hoss. Nothin' else could make him look like that."

"No. I just got back my girl," replied Pan gaily.

"Gurl! Say, cowboy," began Blinky in consternation, "you didn't run foul of that little Yellow Mine Kid?"

"Eat your supper, you hungry-looking galoot," replied Pan. "And you, too, Gus. Because if I begin to shoot off my chin now, you'll forget the grub."

Thus admonished, and with curious glances at Pan, the cowboys took his advice and attacked the generous meal Lying Juan set before them. Their appetites attested to a strenuous day. Pan did not seem to be hungry, which fact caused Juan much concern.

"A-huh! It's the way a fellar gets when he's in love with a gurl," observed the keen Blinky. "I ben there."

After supper they got together before the stove and rolled their cigarettes. The cold night wind, with its tang of mountain heights, made the fire most agreeable. Pan spread his palms to the heat.

"Wal, pard, throw it off your chest before you bust," Blinky advised shrewdly.

"What kind of a day did you boys have?" countered Pan with a laugh.

"Good an' bad," replied Gus, while Blinky shook his head. "Some hoss thieves have been runnin' off our stock. We had some fine hosses, not broke yet. Some we wanted to keep."

"What's the good news?" queried Pan.

"Pan, I'll be dog-goned if we didn't see a million broomies today," burst out Blinky.

"No. Now, Blink, talk sense. You mean you saw a thousand?"

"Wal, shore a million is stretchin' it some," acknowledged the cowboy. "But ten thousand wouldn't be nothin'. We tracked some of our hosses twenty miles an' more over heah, farther'n we'd been yet. We climbed a high ridge an' looked down into the purtiest valley I ever seen. Twice as big as Hot Springs Valley. Gee, it lay there gray an' green with hosses as thick as greasewood bushes on the desert. Thet valley hasn't been drove yet. It's purty rough gettin' up to where you can see. An' there's lots of hosses closer to town. Thet accounts."

"Blinky, is this talk of yours a leaf out of Lying Juan's book?" Pan asked incredulously. "It's too good to be true."

"Pan, I'd swear it on a stack of Bibles," protested Blinky. "Ask Gus."

"For oncet Blinky ain't out of his haid," corroborated Hans. "Never saw so many wild hosses. An' if we can find a way to ketch some of them, we'll be rich."

"Boys, you told me you'd been trapping horses at the water holes," said Pan.

"Shore, we've been moonshinin' them," replied Blinky. "We build a corral 'round a water hole. Make a wide gate we can shut quick. Then we lay out on moonlight nights waitin' for 'em to come in to drink. We've done purty darn' good at it, too."

"That's fun, but it's a two-bit way to catch wild horses," rejoined Pan.

"Wal, they're all doin' it thet way. Hardman's outfit, an' a couple more besides us. I figgered myself it was purty slow, but no better way come to me. Do you know one?"

"Do I? Well, I should smile. I know more than one that'll beat your moonshining. Back on the prairie, where it's all wide and bare, there's no chance for a small outfit. But this is high country, valleys, cañons, cedars. Boys, we can make one big stake before the other outfits get on to us."

"By gosh, one's enough for us," declared Blinky. "Then we can shake this gold claim country where they steal your empty tin cans an' broken shovels."

"One haul will do me, too," agreed Pan. "Then Arizona for me."

"A-huh! Pan, how about this gurl?"

Briefly then Pan told his story, and the situation as it looked to him at the moment. The response of these cowboys was what he had expected. He knew them. Warm-hearted, simple, elemental, they responded in different ways, but with the same fire. Gus Hans looked his championship while Blinky raved and swore.

"Then you're both with me?" asked Pan tersely. "Mind, it's no fair deal, my getting your support here for helping you with a wild horse drive."

"Fair!" Blinky returned forcibly. "It ain't like you to insult cowboys."

"I'm begging your pardon," replied Pan. "But we'd never been pardners, and I hesitated to draw you into a scrap that'll almost sure go to gun throwing."

"Wal, we're your pardners now, an' proud of it, Pan-handle Smith."

Silently and grimly they all shook hands on it. Not half a

dozen times in his range life had Pan been party to a compact like that.

"This Blake fellar, now," began Blinky. "What's your idea of gettin' him out?"

"I want a horse, a blanket, some grub and a gun. I'm to take them down to the jail at eleven o'clock."

"Huh! Goin' to hold up the guard?" queried Blinky.

"That was my intention," replied Pan, "but I know that fellow Hurd, who'll be on guard then. I'll not have to hold him up."

"Hurd? I know him. Hard nut, but I think he's square."

"Reckon Hurd will lose his job," Pan said reflectively. "If he does, let's take him with us on the wild horse deal."

"Suits me. An' he'll shore love thet job. Hurd hasn't any use for Matthews."

"Blinky, do you know another man we can hire or get to throw in with us? We've got five now, counting my dad, and we'll need at least six."

"Let's get thet miner, Charley Brown."

"But he's working a gold claim."

"Wal, if I know anythin', he'll not be workin' it any longer than findin' blue dirt. Gus an' me seen Jard Hardman with two men ridin' out thet way this mawnin'."

"Ah! So Hardman is here now. We'll hunt up Brown and see what he says. Suppose we walk downtown now."

Being early in the evening, the Yellow Mine was not yet in full swing. The dance was on with a few heavy-footed miners and their gaudy partners, and several of the gambling tables were surrounded.

Pan stalked about alone. His new-found cowboy friends had been instructed to follow him unobtrusively. Pan did not wish to give an impression that he had taken up with allies.

He was looking for Charley Brown, but he had a keen roving eye for every man in sight. He took up a position, presently, behind one of the poker games, with his back to the wall, so that he had command of the room.

Gradually more men came in, the gaming tables filled up, and the white-armed girls appeared to mingle with the guests.

Pan espied the girl, Louise, before she had become aware of his presence. She appeared to be more decently clad, a circumstance that greatly added to her charm, in Pan's opinion. Curiously he studied her. Women represented more to Pan than to most men he had had opportunity to meet or observe. He never forgot that they belonged to the same sex as his mother. So it was natural he had compassion for this unsexed dance-hall, gambling-lure girl. She was pretty in a wild sort of way, not in any sense weak. A terrible havoc showed in her face for anyone with eyes to see beneath the surface. Her hawk-like eyes did not miss anyone there, and finally they located him.

She came around the tables, up to Pan, and took hold of his arm.

"Howdy, handsome," she said, smiling up at him. "Didn't I warn you not to come back?"

"Yes, but I thought you were only fooling. Besides, I *had* to come."

"Why? You don't fit here. You've got too clean a look."

Pan gazed down at her, feeling in her words and presence something that prompted him to more than kindliness and good nature.

"Louise, I can return the compliment. You don't fit here."

"Curse you!" she flashed. "I'll fall in love with you."

"Well, if you did, I'd sure drag you out of this hell," replied Pan bluntly.

"Come away from these gamblers," she demanded, and drew him from behind the circle of seats to an empty table. "I won't ask you to drink or dance. But I'm curious. You're Panhandle Smith, aren't you?"

"Reckon so. Who told you?"

"I overheard Dick Hardman tonight, just before supper. He has a room next to mine in the hotel here, when he stays in town. He was telling his father about you. Such cussing I never heard. I'm giving you a hunch. They'll do away with you."

"Thanks. Reckon it's pretty fine of you to put me on my guard."

"I only meant behind your back. What has Dick got against you?"

"We were kids together back in Texas. Just natural rivals and enemies. But I hadn't seen him for years till last night. Then he didn't know me."

"He knows you now, all right. He ran into you today."

"I reckon he did," replied Pan with a grim laugh.

"Panhandle, this is getting sort of warm," she said, leaning across the table to him. "I'm not prying into your affairs. But I could be your friend. . . . I didn't hear all Dick said. When he talked loud, he cussed. But I heard enough to tie up Panhandle Smith with this girl, Lucy, and the Hardman outfit."

Pan eyed her steadily. She was encroaching upon sacred ground. But her feeling was genuine, and undoubtedly she had some connection with a situation that began to look complex. Regardless of circumstances, he knew when to grasp an opportunity.

"Louise, you show you'd risk taking a chance on me . . . a stranger," he replied with quick decision. "I return that compliment."

The smile she gave him was really a reward. It gave him a glimpse of the depths of her.

"Who's this girl Lucy?" she queried.

"She's my sweetheart, ever since we were kids," returned Pan with emotion. "I went to riding the ranges, and well, like so many cowboys, I didn't go back home. When I did go, Lucy was gone . . . my family was gone. I trailed them here . . . to find that Dick Hardman was about to force Lucy to marry him."

She burst out in wrathful denunciation. Then after her excitement cooled: "How'd he aim to force her?"

Quickly Pan explained the situation as related to Jem Blake.

"Aha! Easy to savvy. That's where Jard Hardman and Matthews come in. Panhandle, they're a dirty outfit . . . and the dirtiest of them is Dick Hardman!" the girl exclaimed.

"What's he to you, Louise?" Pan inquired gravely. "You'll excuse me if I say I can't see you in love with him."

"In love with Dick Hardman?" she whispered hotly. "I wouldn't soil even my hands on him . . . if I didn't have to. . . . He met me in Frisco. He brought me to this rotten hole. He made me promises he never kept. He has double-crossed me. And I *had* to sink to this! Drink? Yes, sure I drink. Don't you understand I have to drink to stand this life? I haven't been drinking yet because you got here early. Something deep must be behind my meeting you, Panhandle Smith."

"I hope to heaven it will be to your good . . . as I know meeting you will be to mine," replied Pan fervently.

"We're off the track," she broke in, and Pan imagined he saw a deeper red under her artificial color. "I despise Dick Hardman. He's stingy, conceited, selfish. He's low-down, and he's sinking to worse."

"His father ruined mine," Pan told her. "That's what brought Dad out here . . . to try to get something back from Jard Hardman. But it was no use. He only got another hard deal."

"That cowboy who was in here with you last night . . . Blinky Moran. His claim was jumped by Hardman."

"Louise, how'd you know that?" asked Pan in surprise.

"Don't give me away. Blinky told me. He's one of my friends, and he's a white man if I ever saw one. He has been in love with me. Wanted me to marry him. Poor crazy boy. I sure had to fight to keep from more than liking him. He spent all his money on me, and I had to make him quit."

"Well, that little bowlegged cowboy liar! He's as deep as the sea."

"Keep it secret, Panhandle," she responded seriously. "I don't want to hurt his feelings. . . . To get back to the Hardmans. They've taken strong hold here. The old man owns half of Marco. He's in everything. But it's my hunch I'm giving you . . . that he's in the straight deals only to cover the crooked ones. That's where the money is."

"Yet Jard Hardman will not square up with Dad!" exclaimed Pan.

"Now tell me why you came into the Yellow Mine. You're taking an awful chance. Every night or so some tipsy miner gets robbed or knifed or shot."

"Louise, in dealing with men of really dangerous quality your only chance is to face them with precisely the same thing. As for the four-flushers like Matthews, and men of the Hardman stamp, the one thing they can't stand is nerve. They haven't got it. They don't understand it. They fear it. It works on their consciousness. They begin to figure on what the nervy man means to do before they do anything. . . . If I did not show myself in the street, and here, the Hardman outfit would soon run true to their deals. So by appearing to invite and seek a fight, I really avoid one."

"So that's why they call you Panhandle Smith?" queried the girl meditatively. "I mean with the tone old man Hardman used. They call me Angel. But that doesn't mean what it sounds, does it?"

"I can't figure you, Louise," Pan said dubiously.

"I'm glad you can't. Hello, there's Blinky and his pard, Gus. What're they up to?"

"They are looking pretty hard, but it can't be for you and me. They saw us long ago."

"There! Hardman and Matthews, coming from behind the bar. There's a private office in behind. You can see the door. . . . Panhandle, let me tell you Hardman seldom shows up here."

Pan leisurely got to his feet. His eye quickly caught Matthews's black sombrero, then the big ham of a face, with its drooping mustache. Then Pan perceived that Matthews's companion was a stout man, bearded, dressed like a prosperous rancher.

With deft movement he hitched his belt round farther forward on his hip. It was careless, it might have been accidental, but it was neither. And the girl grasped its meaning. She turned white under her paint, and the eyes that searched Pan's were just then like any other woman's.

"Stop," she called low after him. "You smilin' devil!"

Pan moved leisurely in among the tables, toward the bar and the two men standing rather apart from the crowd. He maneuvered so that Matthews's roving glance fell upon him. Then Pan advanced straight. He saw the sheriff start, then speak hurriedly to Hardman.

Pan halted within six feet of both men. He might never have seen Jard Hardman so far as any recognition was concerned. He faced a man of about fifty years of age, rather florid of complexion, well-fed and used to strong drink.

"Excuse me," Pan spoke with most consummate coolness, addressing the shorter man. Apparently he did not see Matthews. "Are you Jard Hardman?"

"Reckon I am, if that's any of your business," came a gruff reply. Light, hard, speculative eyes took Pan in from head to foot.

"Do you recognize me?" asked Pan in the same tone.

"No, sir, I never saw you in my life," retorted Hardman. And he turned away.

Pan made a step. His long arm shot out, and his hand, striking Hardman's shoulder, whirled him round.

"My name's Smith!" Pan called in vibrant loud voice that stilled the room. "Panhandle Smith!"

"I don't know you, sir," replied Hardman, aghast and amazed. He began to redden. He turned to Matthews, as if in wonder that this individual permitted him to be thus affronted.

"Well, you knew my dad . . . to his loss," declared Pan. "And that's my business with you."

"You've no business with me," Hardman fumed in rising anger.

"Reckon you're mistaken," went on Pan slowly and easily. "I'm Bill Smith's boy. And I mean to have an accounting with you on that Texas cattle deal."

These deliberate words, heard by all within earshot, caused little less than a deadlock throughout the room. The bartenders quit, the drinkers poised glasses in air, the voices suddenly hushed. Pan had an open space behind him, a fact he was responsible for. He faced Matthews, Hardman, and then the length of the bar. He left the gamblers behind to Blinky and Gus, who stood to one side. Pan had invited an argument with the owner of the Yellow Mine and his sheriff ally. Every Westerner in the room understood its meaning.

"You upstart cowpuncher!" Hardman presently shouted. "Get out of here or I'll have you arrested."

"Arrest me? What for? I'm only asking you for an honest deal. I can prove you cheated my father out of cattle. You can't arrest me for that."

"I'll . . . I'll . . . ," choked Hardman, his body leaping with rage, his face growing purple under his beard. Then he turned to Matthews. "Throw this drunk cowboy out."

That focused attention upon the sheriff. Pan read in Matthews's eyes the very things he had suspected, and, as he relaxed the mental and muscular strain under which he had waited, he laughed in Matthews's face.

"Bah! Hardman, you're backed by the wrong man. And at last you've run into the wrong man. Haven't you sense enough to see that? You cheated my father. Now you're going to make it good."

Hardman, furious and imperious, never grasped the significance that had frozen Matthews. Yielding to rage, he yelled at Pan: "Bill Smith sicced his cowpuncher on me, hey! Like father, like son! You're a rustler breed. I'll drive you. . . ."

Pan leaped like a tiger and struck Hardman with a terrible blow in the face. Like something thrown from a catapult, he went into the crowd next the bar, and, despite this barrier and the hands grasping at his flying arms, he crashed to the floor.

But, even before he fell, Pan had leaped back in the same position he had held in front of Matthews.

"He lied!" cried Pan. "My dad, Bill Smith, was as honest a cattleman as ever lived! Mister Sheriff, do you share that slur cast on him?"

"I don't know Bill Smith," Matthews replied hastily. "Reckon I'm not talkin' ag'in' men I don't know. An' as I'm not armed, I can't argue with a gun-packin' cowboy."

Thus he saved his face with the majority of those present. But he did have a gun. Pan knew that as well as if he had seen it. Matthews was not the "even break" stripe of sheriff.

"A-huh!" Pan ejaculated sardonically. "All right. Then I'll be looking for you to arrest me next time we meet."

"I'll arrest you, Panhandle Smith, you can gamble on thet," declared Matthews harshly.

"Arrest nothing," replied Pan with ringing scorn. "You're a four-flush sheriff. I'll gamble you elected yourself. I know your kind, Matthews. And I'll gamble some more that you don't last long in Marco."

This was, as Pan deliberately intended, raw talk that any man not a coward would not swallow. But Matthews was a coward. That appeared patent to all onlookers, in their whispers and nodding heads. Whatever prestige he had held there in that rough mining community was gone, until he came out to face this fiery cowboy with a gun.

White and shaking, he turned to the group of men who had gotten Hardman to his feet. They led him out the open door, and Matthews followed.

Pan strode back to the table where Louise sat tense and wide-eyed. The hum of voices began again, the clatter of glasses, the clink of coin. The incident had passed.

"Well, little girl, I had them figured, didn't I?" Pan asked, calling a smile to break his tight cold face.

"I don't know . . . what . . . ails me," she said breathlessly. "I see fights every night. And I've seen men killed . . . dragged out. But this got my nerve."

"It wasn't much to be excited about. I didn't expect any fight."

"Your idea was to show up Hardman and Matthews before the crowd. You sure did. The crowd was with you. And so am I, Panhandle Smith." She held out a slim hand. "I've got to dance and drink. Good night."

Chapter Ten

Pan's exit from the Yellow Mine was remarkable for the generous space accorded him by its occupants. He sauntered down into the street, and, as he went, he heard the *jangle* of spurs behind him. Blinky and Gus were covering his rear. Presently they joined him, one on each side.

"Wal, Pan, I was shore in on thet," said Blinky, gripping Pan's arm.

"Say, you called 'em flat," Gus added with a hard note in his voice. "When it come down to hardpan, they wasn't there."

"Pan, you remember me tellin' you about Purcell, who jumped my claim with young Hardman?" queried Blinky. "Wal, Purcell was there, settin' some tables back of where you made your stand. I seen him when we first went in. 'Course, everybody quit playin' cards when you called old Hardman. An' I made it my particular biz to get close to Purcell. He was pullin' his gun under the table when I kicked him. An' when he looked up, he seen somethin', you can bet on thet. Wal, Purcell is one man in Hardman's outfit we'll have to kill. Gus will back me up on thet."

"I shore will. Purcell's a Nevada claim jumper, accordin' to talk. Somebody hinted he belonged to thet Plummer gang thet was cleaned out at Bannock years ago. He's no spring chicken, thet's shore."

94

"Point Purcell out to me the first chance you get," replied Pan. "Don't figure I expect to bluff everybody. It can't be done. Somebody will try me out . . . if only to see what I can do. That's the game, you know."

"Hell, yes. An' all you got to do, Pan, is to be there first."

"Reckon tomorrow will be shore interestin'," remarked Gus.

"That girl Louise gave me a hunch," Pan said thoughtfully. "Struck me she was square. Blink, you've talked to her, of course?"

"Me? Aw . . . couple of times, I reckon. She won't look at me unless she's drinking," Blinky replied, both confused and gloomy.

"You've got Louise figured wrong, cowboy," returned Pan. "I'll prove it to you sometime. Now let's get down to business and figure out our plan for Blake's release from jail. I want us to lead the horse roundabout, so I won't be seen by anybody."

They returned to camp and, replenishing the fire, sat around it talking of the wild horse drive.

About ten o'clock, Blinky went to the corral, saddled a horse, and led it back to the tent. There they put on the blanket and saddlebags. Blinky produced a gun he could spare, and then thoughtfully added a small bag of grain for the horse.

"It's darker'n the mill-tail of Hades," announced Blinky, "an' thet's good fer this kind of work. I'll go ahaid, pickin' out the way, an' you lead the hoss."

So they set out into the night, working along the base of the slope. No stars showed, and the raw wind hinted of rain or snow. The lights of the town shone dimly. Keen on the breeze floated the discordant music and revelry from the Yellow Mine and other like dives in full blast.

Descending the slope required careful slow work. The incline was steep, of soft earth and loose shale. But Blinky knew where to feel his way, and eventually they reached the flat, to find easier progress. Pan kept Blinky's dark, silent, moving form in sight. A dim light grew larger. Then a low flat building loomed up faintly in the gloom.

"Go ahead," whispered Blinky. "I'll hold the hoss."

Pan went swiftly up to the wall, and thence along it to the corner. The light came from an open door. He listened. Luckily Hurd was alone. Pan slipped around the corner and entered. Hurd sat at the table in the flare of a lamp, turned down low.

"Ha! Was waitin' fer you, an' beginnin' to worry," he said in a hoarse whisper.

"Plenty of time, if Blake's all ready," replied Pan.

"I'm givin' you a hunch. He's damn' queer fer a fellar who expects to break jail."

"No matter. Let's get at it *pronto*."

Hurd got up and laid his gun on the table. Then he turned over the bench, threw papers on the floor. "Thar's the key, an' hyar's a rope. Hawg-tie me."

With that he turned his back. Swiftly Pan bound him securely, and let him down upon the floor. Then he unlocked the door, opened it. Pitch darkness inside and no sound! He called in a low voice. Blake did not reply. Muttering in surprise, Pan took the lamp and went into the room. He found Blake asleep, although fully dressed. Pan jerked him roughly out of that indifferent slumber.

"It's Smith," he said bluntly. "You sure must *want* to get out. Hang you, Blake, this whole deal looks fishy to me. Come on."

Leaving the lamp there, Pan dragged the man out, through the dark entrance room. In another moment they had reached the horse and Blinky.

"Here's money and a gun," whispered Pan swiftly. "You'll find grub, blanket, grain on your saddle. Get on!" Pan had to half lift Blake upon the horse. He felt of the stirrups. "They're all right. The road is that way, about fifty yards. Turn to the left and ride. Remember, Siccane."

Blake rode into the darkness without a word.

"Was he drunk?" Blinky queried in a hoarse whisper. "Shore acted funny for a sober man."

"He didn't breathe like he was drunk," replied Pan. "But he flabbergasted me. Found him asleep! And he never said a darned word. Blinky, it sticks in my craw. Reckon he didn't want to leave that nice warm bed."

Morning dawned bright and sparkling. Pan felt a thrill and a longing for the saddle and the open country.

"Wal, reckon this heah'll be our busy day," drawled Blinky, after making a hearty breakfast of bacon and flap-jacks. "Pan, what's first on the ticket?"

"Show me a horse, you bowlegged grub destroyer," Pan replied eagerly.

"Come out to the corral. We got a sorrel as is a real shore enough hoss if you can ride him."

There were a dozen or more horses in the corral.

"Fine string, Blinky," said Pan. "Is that sorrel the one I can't ride?"

"Yes, thet's him. Ain't he a real hoss?"

"Best of the bunch, at first sight. Blinky, are you sure you're not giving me your own horse?"

"Me? I don't care nothin' about him," Blinky declared, lying glibly. "Shore he's the orfullest pitchin' son-of-a-gun I ever forked. But mebbe you can ride him."

It developed presently that Pan could ride the sorrel, and

that Blinky had done the horse a great injustice. How good to be back in the saddle!

"Wal, what's next on the ticket?" queried Blinky.

"I'm going downtown," replied Pan.

"A-huh. I want to trail along with you."

"No, I'll go alone. I'll make my bluff strong, Blinky, or draw Matthews out. Honest, I don't think he'll show."

"Thet yellow dawg? He won't face you, Pan. But he's in thet Hardman outfit, an' one of them . . . mebbe Purcell . . . might take a shot at you from a winder. It's been done heah. Let me go with you."

"Well, if they're that low-down, your being with me wouldn't help much," replied Pan. "Marco is a pretty big place. It's full of men. And Western men are much alike anywhere. Matthews is no fool. He couldn't risk murdering me in broad daylight, from ambush."

"I'm not trustin' him," Blinky said somberly.

Pan strolled down toward the town. A familiar unpleasant mental strain dominated his consciousness. His slow, cool, easy nonchalance was all outward. He hated what his actions meant, what might well ensue from them, yet he was glad it was in him to meet the issue in this way of the West.

His alert faculties of observation belied the leisurely manner of his approach to the main street. He was a keen-strung, watching, listening machine. The lighting and smoking of a cigarette were mechanical pretense—he did not want to smoke.

Two men stood in front of the stage office. One was Jones, the agent. Pan approached them, leaned on the hitching rail. But he favored his right side, and he faced the street.

" 'Mornin', cowboy," Jones greeted him, not without nervousness.

"Howdy, Jones. Can you give me a drink?" returned Pan.

"Sorry, but I haven't a drop."

The other man was an old fellow, although evidently he was still active.

"Tell you, cowboy," he spoke up dryly, "you might buy a bottle at the Yellow Mine."

Pan made no reply, and presently the old man shambled away while Matty Jones entered his office. Pan kept his vigil there, watching, waiting. He was seen by dozens of passing men, but none of them crossed toward the stage office. Down the street straggling pedestrians halted to form little groups. In an hour the business of Marco had apparently halted.

The porch of the Yellow Mine was in plain sight, standing out on a corner scarcely more than a hundred yards down the street. Pan saw Hardman and Matthews come out of the hotel.

They could not fail to observe the quiet, the absence of movement, the waiting knots of men.

This was the climax of strain for Pan. Leisurely he strolled away from the hitching rail, out into the middle of the street. The closer groups of watchers vanished.

Hardman could be seen gesticulating, stamping as if in rage, and then he went into the hotel, leaving Matthews standing alone. Other men, in the background, disappeared. The sheriff stood a moment, irresolute, sagging. Then he wheeled to enter the hotel.

He had damned himself. He had refused the even break, the man-to-man, the unwritten edict of Westerners.

Pan saw this evasion with grim relief. The next move was one easier to perform, although fraught with great peril. Every man in Marco now knew that Pan had come out to meet the men he had denounced. They had been aware of his intention. They had seen him sauntering down the middle of the street. And they had showed what the West called yellow. But they had not showed their claws, if they had any. Pan could well have ended his quest then and there. But to follow it up, to beard the jackals in their den— that was the last word.

As Pan proceeded slowly down the middle of the street, the little groups of spectators disintegrated, and slipped out of sight into the stores and saloons. For a few moments not a single man showed himself. Then they began to reappear behind him, slowly following him.

At the entrance to the Yellow Mine, Pan threw away his cigarette and mounted the steps. He was gambling his life on the code of the Westerners. The big hall-like saloon was vacant except for the two bartenders behind the bar. Pan had heard subdued voices, the shuffle of feet, the closing of doors. Every muscle in his body was cramped with tension, ready to leap like lightning into action. Advancing to the bar he called for a drink.

"On the house this mawnin'," replied the nearest bartender, smiling. Pan took the bottle with his left hand, poured out some liquor, set the bottle down, and lifted the glass. His tension relaxed.

"Sort of quiet this morning," he said.

"Reckon it is, just now," replied the bartender significantly.

"Reckon I might as well move along," Pan remarked, but he did not stir. The bartender went on cleaning glasses. Sounds of footsteps came from outside. Presently Pan walked back through the open door, then halted a moment, to light another cigarette. His back was turned to the bar and the doors. That seemed the climax of his effrontery. It was deliberate, the utter recklessness of the cowboy who had been trained in a hard school. But all that happened was the silence breaking to a gay wild sweet voice: "Come again, cowboy, when there's somebody home!"

Louise had been watching him through some peephole. That had been her tribute to him and her scorn of his opponents.

Pan retraced his steps up the street, finding, as before, a clear passage. Men hailed him from doorways, from windows, from behind obstructions. He did not need to be told that they were with him. Marco had been treated to precisely what it wanted. Pan was quick to grasp the mood of these residents who had been so keen about his endeavor to draw out Hardman and Matthews. That hour saw the beginning of the end for these dominant factors in the evil doings of Marco.

By the time Pan got back to camp his mood actually harmonized with his leisurely free and careless movements. Still he was hiding something, for he wanted to yell. Blinky saw him coming, and yelled for him. The cowboy was beside himself with a frenzy of delight.

In the succeeding hour, leading to noon, what with sundry trips down to the store, the trio learned some news that afforded much satisfaction. Almost everybody, according to the informers, was glad Blake had escaped. It developed that the jail was not a civic institution. Already there had been talk of the permanent citizens getting together.

All this was exceedingly welcome to Pan. He could hardly wait till noon to ride over to his mother's.

On the way out to the farm, halfway beyond the outskirts of town, Pan met his father rushing up the road. At sight of Pan he almost collapsed.

"Just . . . heard . . . the news," he panted.

"Dad, I bluffed them . . . that's all. I believe I got most of the town with me."

"Pan, is it true that you accused Jard Hardman of robbin' me . . . an' you knocked him flat?"

"Sure it's true."

"Lord, but I'd liked to have seen that," Bill Smith declared vehemently. "An', Son, you got Jem Blake out of jail. Bill Dolan, who brought the news, didn't hint you had anythin' to do with that. But I knew. If only Jem does his part!"

"Let's hope he's far on the way to Siccane by now. Does Lucy know? I hope you didn't tell her about my meeting with Hardman and Matthews."

"I didn't. But Dolan shore did," replied his father. "Say, boy, you should have seen Lucy."

"I will see her *pronto*," Pan replied eagerly. "Come on."

Pan walked the horse while his father kept pace alongside.

"Some more news I 'most forgot," he went on. "Dolan told about a shootin' scrape out in Cedar Gulch. Them claim jumpers drove a miner named Brown off his claim. They had to fight for it. Brown said he wounded one of 'em. They chased him to Satler's ranch. Shore wanted to kill him or scare him off for good."

"I know Brown," replied Pan. "And from what he told me, I've a hunch I know the claim jumpers."

"Well, that'd be hard to prove."

"I'll hunt Brown up and persuade him to make the wild horse drive with us. He's. . . ."

"By George, I forgot some more," interrupted Bill Smith, slapping his leg. "Dolan said Wiggett broke with Jard Hardman. Wiggett started this wild hoss buyin' an' shippin' East. Hardman had to get his finger in the pie. Now Wiggett is a big man, an' he has plenty of money. I always heard him well spoken of. Now I'll gamble your callin' Jard Hardman the way you did had a lot to do with Wiggett's break with him."

"Shouldn't wonder," rejoined Pan. "And it's darned good luck for us. The boys run across a valley full of wild horses over here about twenty miles. Dad, I believe I can trap several thousand wild horses."

"No!" ejaculated his father.

"If the boys aren't loco, I sure can," Pan declared positively. "Before the snow flies, we will be on the way south to Siccane."

"Lord! I'm a younger man than I was a few days ago. Before the snow flies? That's hardly another month. Pan, how'll we travel?"

"Wagons and horseback. We can buy wagon outfits for next to nothing. There's a corral full of them at Black's. Second-hand, but good enough."

"Mother an' Lucy will be glad. They hate this country."

"There! Isn't that Lucy at the gate now?" suddenly queried Pan.

"Reckon it is," replied his father. "Ride ahead, Son. I'll take my time."

Pan urged the sorrel into a lope, then a gallop, and from that to a run. In just a few rods Pan took the measure of this splendid horse. Swift, strong, sure-footed, and easy-gaited, and betraying no sign of a mean spirit, the sorrel won Pan.

Lucy waved to Pan as he came clattering down the road. Then she disappeared in the green foliage. Leading his horse, he hurried in toward the house, looking everywhere. The girl, however, was not to be seen.

He dropped his bridle, and mounted the porch to embrace his mother, who met him with suppressed emotions. Her hands were more expressive than her words.

"Oh, I'm all here, Mother." He laughed. "Where's Lucy?"

"Lucy ran through the house like a whirlwind," replied his mother with a smile. "The truth is, my son, she has been quite beside herself since she heard of her father's release from jail. You'll find her in the orchard or down by the brook."

Pan did not seek Lucy in the orchard. Leaping upon the sorrel, he loped down the sandy hard-packed path toward the brook and the shady tree with its bench. Pan knew she would be there. Dodging the overhanging branches, he kept peering through the aisles of green for a glimpse of white or a golden head. Suddenly he was rewarded. Lucy stood in the middle of the sunny glade.

Pan rode to her side and leaped from the saddle. Her face was pale, and wet with tears. But her eyes were now dry, wide and purple, radiant with unutterable gladness. She rushed into his arms.

Chapter Eleven

Before dark that night Pan had most of his preparations made, so that next morning there would be nothing to do but eat, pack the horses, saddle up, and ride.

At suppertime Charley Brown and MacNew, alias Hurd, called at the camp. The latter was a little the worse for the bottle.

The outcome of that visit was the hiring of both men to go on the wild horse drive. Brown's claim had been jumped by strangers. It could not be gotten back without a fight. Brown had two horses and a complete outfit; MacNew had only the clothes on his back.

"Fired me 'thout payin' my wages," he said sullenly.

"Who fired you, Mac?" inquired Pan.

"Hardman!" MacNew replied with a bitter oath.

Brown had an interesting account to give of his meeting with Dick Hardman down at the Yellow Mine. The young scion of the would-be dictator of Marco's fortunes had raved about what he would do to Panhandle Smith.

Pan tried to laugh it off, but Blinky manifestly had seen red at the mention of Dick Hardman's name. Drawing the irate cowboy aside, Pan inquired kindly and firmly: "It's because of Louise?"

"Naw," replied Blinky, averting his face.

"Don't you lie to me, Blinky," went on Pan earnestly,

shaking the cowboy. "I've guessed your trouble, and I'm your friend."

"Wal, Pan, I'm darn' glad an' lucky if you're my friend," said Blinky. "But what trouble are you hintin' about?"

Pan whispered: "You're in love with Louise."

"What if I am?" Blinky hissed in fierce shame. "Are you holdin' thet ag'in' me?"

"No, I'm hanged if I don't like you better for it."

That was too much for Blinky. He gazed mutely up at Pan. Pan never saw such eyes of misery.

"Blinky, that girl is wicked," went on Pan. "But that's only the drink. She couldn't carry on that life without drinking. She told me so. There's something great about that little girl. I believe she could be made into a good woman. Why don't you try it? I'll help you. She likes you. She told me that, too."

"But Louise won't ever see me unless she's drinking," protested Blinky.

"That's proof. She doesn't want you wasting your time and money at the Yellow Mine. She thinks you're too good for that . . . when she's sober. Talk straight now, Blinky. You do love her, bad as she is?"

"So help me, I do!" burst out the cowboy abjectly. "It's purty near killed me. The more I see of her, the more I care. I'm so sorry fer her I can't stand it. Dick Hardman fetched her out heah from Frisco. Wal, he never cared nothin' fer her, an' she hates him. She swears she'll kill him. An' I'm afraid she'll do it. Thet's why I'd like to stick a gun into him."

"Marry Louise. Take her away. Come south with us to Arizona," replied Pan.

"Pardner, you're too swift fer me," Blinky whispered huskily, and he clutched Pan. "Would you let us go with you?"

"Sure. Why not? Lucy and my mother know nothing

about Louise. I'd rather not tell them, but I wouldn't be afraid to."

"But Louise won't marry me."

"If we can't talk her into it when she's sober, by heaven, we'll get her some other way. Now, Blinky, it's settled. With some money we can figure on homes far from this bitter country . . . *homes,* cowboy, do you savvy that? With cattle and horses . . . some fine open grassy rolling country . . . where nobody ever heard of Blinky Moran and Panhandle Smith."

"Pard, it ain't my right name," mumbled Blinky. He was crying.

"No difference," Pan replied, holding the boy tightly a moment. "Brace up, now, Blinky. It's all settled."

Pan left the cowboy there in the darkness, and returned to camp. He had known more than one good-for-nothing cowboy, drinking and gambling himself straight to hell, who had fooled his detractors and had taken the narrow trail for a woman deemed worthless. There was something about this kind of fight that appealed to Pan. As for the girl, Louise Melliss, and her reaction to such a desperate climax, Pan had only his strange faith that it might create a revolution in her soul. At least he was absolutely sure she would never return to such a life.

Pan sought his blankets very late, and it seemed he scarcely had closed his eyes when Juan called him. It was pitch dark outside. The boys were stirring, the campfire crackling. He smelled the frying ham, the steaming coffee.

" 'Mawnin', pardner," drawled Blinky. "Shore thought you was daid. Grab a pan of grub heah. An' say, cowboy, from now on you can call me Somers . . . Frank Somers. I'm proud of the name, but I reckon it was ashamed of me."

"A-huh. All right, Blinky Somers," Pan replied cheerfully.

"You'll always be Blinky to me."

They ate standing or sitting before the campfire, in the chill blackness just beginning to turn gray. Then swift hands went at beds and packs, horses and saddles. When dawn broke, the hunters were on their way, far up the cedar slope.

Blinky was first, leading a pack horse, Pan followed next, and the four other men strung out behind, with bobbing pack horses between. This ridge was the high ground between Marco Valley and Hot Springs Valley. Soon the trail led down. The rising sun killed the chill in the air, and, by the time the hunters had reached level ground again, it was hot.

They rode across the valley, which appeared to be five or six miles wide, to begin ascending another slope. They climbed and crossed that ridge, which could have been called a foothill if there had been any mountains near. Another valley, narrow and rough, not so low as the last, lay between this ridge and the next one, a cedared rise of rock and yellow earth that promised hard going. Climbing it was difficult.

It was rather a wide-topped ridge, and not until Pan had reached an open break on the far side could he see what kind of country lay beyond.

"Wal, there she is, my wild hoss valley," said Blinky, who sat his horse alongside of Pan. "An', by golly, thet's the name for her, Wild Hoss Valley."

Pan nodded his acquiescence. In truth he had been rendered quite speechless by the wildness and beauty of the scene below and beyond him. A valley yawned beneath, so deep and wide that it appeared like a blue lake, so long that he could only see the north end, which notched under a rugged mountain slope, green and black and golden and white.

The height upon which he stood was the last of the ridges, for the elevation that lay directly across was a noble range of foothills, timbered, cañoned, apparently insurmountable for horses.

But it was the blue floor of the valley that longest held Pan's enraptured gaze. It looked level, although to an experienced eye that was deceitful. Grass and sage! What were the innumerable colored rocks or bushes or dots that covered the floor of the valley? They were wild horses!

At near the sunset hour, the journey was ended. The slope they had descended ran out into an immense buttress jutting far into the valley. A low brushy arm of the incline extended out half a mile to turn toward the main slope and to break off short, leaving a narrow opening out into the valley. The place was not only ideal for a hidden campsite, with plenty of water, grass, wood, but also for such a wild horse trap as Pan had in mind.

"How wide is that gap?" asked Pan.

"Reckon it cain't be more'n the length of two lassoes," replied Blinky.

"Rope it off high, boys, and turn the stock loose. This corral was made for us," Pan instructed enthusiastically.

Dusk settled down into this neck of the great valley. Coyotes barked out in the open. From the heights pealed down the mournful, blood-curdling, yet beautiful bay of a wolf.

Pan had to attempt to answer a hundred queries. Finally he lost patience.

"Say, you long-eared jackasses," he exploded, "I tell you it all depends on the lay of the land! I mean the success of a big drive. If 'round the corner, here, there's good running ground . . . well, it'll be great for us. We'll look the ground over and size up the valley for horses. Find where they water and graze. If we decide to use this place as a trap to drive into, we'll throw up two blind corrals just inside that gateway out there.

Then we'll throw a fence of cedars as far across the valley as we can drag cedars. The farther the better. It'll have to be a fence too thick and high for horses to break through or jump over. That means work. When that's done, we'll go up the valley, get behind the wild horses, and drive them down."

Loud, indeed, were the commendations showered upon Pan's plan.

Chapter Twelve

Pan's father was an early riser, and next morning he routed everybody out before the clear white morning star had gone down in the velvet-blue sky.

Blinky later accompanied Pan to the ridge that they climbed at a point opposite camp. Probably it was four or five hundred feet high, and provided a splendid prospect of the valley. Pan could scarcely believe his eyes. He saw wild horses, so many that for the time being he forgot the other important details. He counted thirty bands in a section of the valley no more than fifteen miles long and less than half as wide.

He gazed and gazed. From near to far the bands dotted the green-gray valley. Far away this valley floor shaded into blue. Near at hand the colors were easily distinguishable. Blacks and bays, whites and chestnuts, pintos that resembled zebras, dotted this wild pasture land. The closest band to where Pan and Blinky stood could not have been more than a mile distant, in a straight line.

But a million wild horses in sight would be of no marketable value if they could not be trapped. So Pan bent his keen gaze here and there, up and down the valley, across to the far side, and upon the steep wall nearby.

"Blink, see that deep wash running down the valley? It looks a good deal closer to the far side. That's a break in the valley floor, all right. It may be a wonderful help to us, and it may ruin our chances. But I'm almost sure it's a deep wide wash, with steep walls. Impassable! And, by golly, if that's so . . . you're a rich cowboy."

"Haw! Haw! Gosh, the way you sling words around."

"Now let's work along this ridge."

At length Pan and Blinky arrived at the extreme end of the cape-like bluff. It stood higher than their first look-out.

Pan, who arrived at a vantage point ahead of Blinky, immediately let out a stentorian yell. Whereupon his companion came running.

"Hey, what's eatin' you?" he panted.

"Look!" exclaimed Pan.

The steep yellow slope opposite them, very close at the point where the bluff curved in, stretched away almost to the other side of the valley. Indeed, it constituted the southern wall of the valley, and was broken only by the narrow pass below where the cowboys stood, and another wider break at the far end. From this point the wash that had puzzled Pan proved to be almost a cañon in dimensions. It kept to the lowest part of the valley floor and turned to run parallel with the slope.

"Blink, suppose we run a fence of cedars from the slope straight out to the wash. Reckon that's two miles and more. Then close up any gaps along this side of the valley. What would happen?"

Blinky spat out his cigarette.

"You dog-gone wild hoss wrangler!" he ejaculated with starting eyes and healthy grin. "Shore I begin to get your hunch. A blind man could figure this deal heah. Big corrals hid behind the gate under us . . . long fence out there to the wash . . . close up any holes on this side of valley . . . then make a humdinger of a drive. Cowboy, shore's you're born

I'm seein' my Arizona ranch right this minnit!"

"Reckon I'm seeing things, too," Pan agreed in suppressed excitement. "Blink, is there *any* mistake?"

"What about?"

"The market for wild horses."

"Absolutely, no," declared Blinky vehemently. "It's new. Only started last summer. Wiggett made money. He said so. Thet's what fetched the Hardmans nosin' into the game. Mebbe this summer will kill the business, but right now we're safe. We can sell all the hosses we can ketch, right heah on the hoof, without breakin' or drivin'. It's only a day's ride from Marco, or we can drive to the railroad. I'd say sell at ten dollars a haid right heah an' whoop."

"I should smile," replied Pan. "It'll take us ten days or more, working like beavers to cut and drag the cedars to build that fence. More time if there are gaps to close along this side. Then all we've got to do is to drive the valley. One day will do it. Why, I never saw or heard of such a trap. You can bet it will be driven only once. The wild horses we don't catch will steer clear of this valley. But breaking a big drove, or driving them to Marco . . . it'd take a month, even with a small herd."

"Hardman an' Wiggett have several outfits working, mebbe fifty riders all told. They've been handlin' hosses. Reckon Wiggett would jump at buyin' up a thousand haid, all he could get. He's from Saint Louis an' what he knows about wild hosses ain't a lot."

"Blinky, old-timer, we've got the broomics sold. It'll be too easy. It makes me afraid."

"Thet somethin' unforeseen will happen, huh?" Blinky queried shrewdly. "I had the same idee."

"But what could happen?" asked Pan, darkly speculative.

"We'll work ourselves till we're daid in our boots. Then

we'll drive . . . drive them wild hosses as hosses was never drove before."

"Well, what then?" queried Pan.

"Drive 'em right in heah where Hardman's outfit will be waitin'!"

"Such a thing couldn't happen," Pan flashed hotly.

"Wal, it just could," drawled Blinky, "an' we couldn't do a thing but fight."

"Fight?" repeated Pan passionately.

"Thet's what I said, pard," replied his comrade coolly. "An' it shore would be one fight, with all the best of numbers an' guns on Hardman's side. We've got only three rifles besides our guns, an' not much ammunition. I fetched all we had, an' sent Gus for more. But Black didn't send thet over, an' I forgot to go after it.'

"We can send somebody back to Marco," Pan said broodingly. "Say, you've given me a shock. I never thought of such a possibility. I see now it *could* happen, but the chances are a thousand to one against it."

On the way back to camp, Pan, pondering very gravely over the question, at last decided that such a bold raid was a remote possibility, and that his and Blinky's subtle reaction to the thought came from their highly excited imaginations.

"Let's see," he asked when he reached camp, "how many horses have we, all told?"

"Thirty-one, countin' the pack hosses, an' thet outlaw sorrel of yours," replied Blinky.

"Reckon we'll have to ride them all. Dragging cedars pulls a horse down."

In due time all the horses were ridden and driven back to camp, where a temporary corral had been roped off.

"Now, men, we're ready to look the valley over," said Pan. "I'll take Dad with me. Blink, you and Gus turn the corner here and keep close under the slope all the way up the valley. Look out for places where the wild horses might climb out. Charley, you and MacNew cross to the other side of the valley, if you can. Look the ground over along that western wall. And everybody keep your eyes peeled for wild horses, so we can get a line on numbers."

They rode out through the gateway into the valley, where they separated into pairs. Pan, with his father, headed south along the slope. He found distances somewhat greater than he had estimated from the bluff, and obstacles that he had not noted at all. But by traveling farther down, he discovered a low ledge of rock, quite a wall in places, that zigzagged out from the slope for a goodly distance. It had breaks here and there that could be easily closed up with brush. This wall would serve very well for part of the fence, and from the end of it out to the wash there was comparatively level ground.

The wash proved to be a perpendicularly walled gorge fifty or more feet deep with a sandy dry floor. It wound somewhat west by north up the valley.

"Dad, there are likely to be side washes or cuts up toward the head, where horses could get down," said Pan. "We'll fence right across here. So if we do chase any horses into the wash, we'll stop them here. Sure, this long hole would make a great trap."

Pan had been deceived in his estimate of the size of the valley. They rode ten miles west before they began to get into rougher ground, scaly with broken rock, and gradually failing in vegetation. The notch of the west end loomed up, ragged and brushy, evidently a wild jumble of cliffs, ledges, timber, and brush. The green patch at the foot meant water and willows. Pan left his father while he rode on five miles farther.

115

The ascent of the valley was like a bowl.

The time came when he gazed back and down over the whole valley. Before him lines and dots of green, widely scattered, told of more places where water ran. Strings of horses moved to and fro, so far away that they were scarcely distinguishable. Beyond these points no horses could be seen. The wash wound like a black ribbon out of sight. The vast sloping lines of valley swept majestically down from the wooded bluff-like sides. It was an austere, gray hollow of the earth.

When they rode into the gateway, the day was far spent, and the west was darkly ablaze with subdued fire.

By the time Lying Juan had supper ready, Blinky and Gus rode into camp.

"Hungrier'n a wolf," said Blinky.

"Well, what's the verdict?" asked Pan.

"Wuss an' more of it,' drawled Blinky. "We seen most five thousand hosses, an' I'll be dog-goned if I don't believe we'll ketch them all. I reckon the valley is a made-to-order corral."

"Blink, you have some intelligence, after all," Pan replied chaffingly.

Early next morning the labor began and proceeded with the utmost dispatch. The slope resounded with the ring of axes. Pan's father was a capital hand at chopping down trees, and he kept two horsemen dragging cedars at a lively rate. The work progressed rapidly, but the fence did not seem to grow in proportion.

In the succeeding days Pan paced up the work, from dawn until dark. A week more saw the long fence completed. It was an obstacle few horses could leap.

Following the completion of the fence, they built a barrier across the wash. And then, to make doubly sure, Pan divided his party into three couples, each to close all possible exits along the branches of the wash and the sides of the slope.

During the latter part of this work the bands of wild horses moved farther westward. But so far as Pan could tell, none left the valley. They had appeared curious and wary, then had moved out of sight over the ridges in the center of the great oval.

That night when they had finished, with two weeks of unremitting toil in dust and heat behind them, was one for explosive satisfaction.

The hunters stayed up later than usual, and had to be reminded twice by Pan of the strenuous morrow.

When he made for his own bed, MacNew followed him in the darkness.

"Smith, I'd like a word with you," said the outlaw under his breath.

"Sure, Mac, glad to hear you," replied Pan, not without a little shock.

"I've stuck on hyar, haven't I?"

"You sure have. I wouldn't ask a better worker. And if the drive is all I hope for, I'll double your money."

"Wal, I didn't come to you on my own hook," rejoined the other hurriedly. "Leastways, it wasn't my idee. Hardman got wind of your hoss trappin' scheme. Thet was after he'd fired me without my wages. Then he sent for me, an' he offered me gold to get a job with you an' keep him posted if you ketched any big bunch of hosses."

Here the outlaw clinked gold coin in his coat pocket.

"I took the gold, an' said I'd do it," MacNew went on deliberately. "But I never meant to double-cross you, an' I haven't. Reckon I might have told you before. It jest didn't come, though, till tonight."

"Thanks, Mac," returned Pan, extending his hand to the outlaw. "I wasn't afraid to trust you. Hardman's playing a high hand then?"

117

"Reckon he is, an' thet's a hunch."

"All right, Mac. I'm thinking you're square with me," replied Pan.

After the outlaw left, Pan sat on his bed pondering this latest phase of the situation. If his wild horse expedition had not reached the last day, he would have sent Blinky back to Marco or have gone himself to see if Hardman's riders could be located. But that was too late. Pan could not postpone the drive, come what might.

Chapter Thirteen

The morning star was going down in an intense dark blue sky when the seven men rode out upon their long-planned drive. The valley was a great obscure void, gray, silent, betraying nothing of its treasure to the hunters. They crossed the wash below the fence, where they had dug entrance and exit, and turned west at a brisk trot. Daylight came lingeringly. The valley cleared of opaque light. Like a gentle rolling sea, it swept away to west and north, divided by its thin dark line, and faintly dotted by bands of wild horses.

In the eastern sky, over the far low gap where the valley failed, the pink light deepened to rose, and then to red. A disk of golden fire tipped the bleak horizon. The whole country became transformed as if with life. The sun had risen on this memorable day for Pan Smith and his father, and for Blinky Somers. Nothing of the black shadows and doubts and fears of night! Pan could have laughed at himself in scorn. Here was the sunrise. How beautiful the valley! There were the wild horses grazing near and far, innumerable hundreds and thousands of them. The thought of the wonderful drive gripped Pan in thrilling fascination. The capture of wild horses would alone have raised him to the heights. How much more tremendous, then, an issue that meant a chance of happiness for all his loved ones.

It was seven o'clock when Pan and his men reached the

western elevation of the valley, something over a dozen miles from their fence and trap. From this vantage point Pan could sweep the whole country with far-sighted eyes. What he saw made them glisten.

Wild horses everywhere, like dots of brush on a bare green rolling prairie!

"Boys, we'll ride down the valley now and pick a place where we split to begin the drive," said Pan.

"Hosses way down there look to me like they was movin' this way," observed Blinky, who had eyes like a hawk.

Pan had keen eyes, too, but he did not believe they could compare with Blinky's. That worthy had the finest of all instruments of human vision—the clear light-gray eye, like that of an eagle. Dark eyes were not so far-seeing on range and desert as the gray or blue. And it was a fact that Pan had to ride down the valley a mile or more before he could detect a movement of wild horses toward him.

"Wal, reckon mebbe thet don't mean nothin'," said Blinky. "An' then again mebbe it does. Hosses run around a lot of their own accord. An' ag'in they get scared of somethin'. If we run into some bunches haidin' this way, we'll turn them back an' thet's work for us."

Pan called a halt there, and, after sweeping his gaze over all the valley ahead, he said: "We split here. . . . Mac, you and Brown ride straight toward the slope. Mac, take a stand a half mile or so out. Brown, you go clear to the slope and build a fire so we can see your smoke. Give us five minutes, say, to see your smoke, and then start the drive. Reckon we'll hold our line all right till they get to charging us. And when we close in down there by the gate, it'll be every man for himself. I'll bet it'll be a stampede."

Pan sent Lying Juan to take up a stand a mile or more outside of MacNew. Gus and Blinky were instructed to place equal distances between themselves and Juan. Pan's father left with them and rode to a ridge top in plain sight a mile away. Pan remained where he had reined his horse.

"Sort of work to them, even to Dad," soliloquized Pan, half amused at his own tremendous boyish eagerness. All his life he had dreamed of some such great experience with horses.

He could see about half the valley floor that was to be driven. The other half lay over the rolling ridges, and obscured by the haze and yellow clouds of dust rising here and there. Those dust clouds had not appeared until the last quarter of an hour or so, and they caused Pan curiosity that almost amounted to anxiety. Surely bands of horses were running.

Suddenly a shot rang out over to Pan's left. His father was waving hat and gun. Far over against the green background of slope curled up a thin column of blue smoke. Brown's signal! In a few moments the drive would be on.

Pan got off to tighten cinches.

"Well, Sorrel, old boy, you look fit for the drive," Pan said, patting the glossy neck. "But I'll bet you'll not be so slick and fat tonight."

When he got astride again, he saw his father and the next driver heading their horses south. So he started Sorrel, and the drive had begun. He waved his sombrero at his father. And he waved it in the direction of home, with a message to Lucy.

Pan rode at a trot. It was not easy to hold in Sorrel. He wanted to go. He scented the wild horses. He knew there was something afoot, and he had been given a long rest. Soon Pan was riding down into one of the shadow depressions, the hollows that gave the valley a resemblance to a ridged sea. Thus he lost sight of the foreground. When, half a mile below, he reached a wave crest of ground, he saw bands of wild horses, enough to make a broken line half across the valley, traveling toward him. They had their heads north, and were moving prettily, probably a couple of miles distant. Beyond them other bands, scattered and indistinct but all in motion, convinced Pan that something had started the horses, or they had sensed the drive.

"No difference now," Pan said aloud. "We're going to run your legs off, and catch the lot of you."

The long black line of horses did not keep intact. It broke into sections, and then into bands, most of which sheered to the left. But one herd of about twenty kept on toward Pan. He halted Sorrel. They came within a hundred yards before they stopped as if frozen. How plump and shiny they were! The lean wild heads and ears all stood up.

A mouse-colored mare was leading this bunch. She whistled shrilly, and then a big roan stallion trotted out from behind. He jumped as if he had been struck and, taking the lead, swung to Pan's left, manifestly to get by him. But they had to run uphill while Pan had only to keep to a level. He turned them before they got halfway to a point even with the next driver. Away they swept, running wild, a beautiful sight, the roan and mare leading, with the others massed behind, manes and tails flying, dust rolling from under their clattering hoofs.

Then Pan turned ahead again, working back toward his place in the driving line. He had a better view here. He saw his father and Gus and Blinky ride toward each other to head off scattered strings of horses. The leaders were too swift for the drivers, and got through the line, but most of the several herds were headed and turned. Gunshots helped to send them scurrying down the valley.

Two small bands of horses appeared coming west along

the wash. Pan loped Sorrel across to intercept them. They were ragged and motley, altogether a score or more of the broomtails that had earned that unflattering epithet. They had no leader and showed it in their indecision. They were as wild as jack rabbits, and, upon sighting Pan, they wheeled in their tracks and fled like the wind, down the valley. Pan saw them turn a larger, darker-colored herd. This feature was what he had mainly relied upon. Wonderful luck of this kind might attend the drive; even a broken line running the right way would sweep the valley front wash to slope. But that was too much for even Pan's most extravagant hopes.

When he had surmounted the next ridge, he faced several miles of almost level valley, with the only perceptible slope toward the left. For the first time he saw all the drivers. They were holding a fairly steady line. As Pan had anticipated, the drive was slowly leading away from the wash, diagonally toward the great basin that constituted the bottom of the valley floor. Bands of horses were running south, bobbing under the dust clouds. There was none within a mile of Pan. The other men, beyond the position of Pan's father, would soon be called upon to do some riding.

As Pan kept on, at a fast trot, he watched in all directions, expecting to see horses come up out of a hollow, or over a ridge; also he took a quick glance every now and then in the direction of his comrades. They were working ahead of him, more and more to the left. Therefore a wide gap soon separated Pan from his father.

This occasioned him uneasiness, because they would soon be down on a level, where palls of dust threatened to close over the whole valley, and it would be impossible to see any considerable distance. If the wild horses then took a notion to wheel and turn back up the valley, the drive would not be prolific of great results.

Pan rode a mile to the left, somewhat uphill and also forward. He caught sight of his father and two other riders, rather far ahead, riding, shooting either behind or in front of a waving pall of dust. The ground down there was dry, and, although covered with grass and sage, it had equally as much bare surface from which the plunging hoofs kicked up the yellow smoke.

Pan had a front of two miles and more to guard, and the distance was increasing every moment. The drive swept to the left, massing toward the apex where the fence and slope met. This was still miles away. Pan could see landmarks he recognized high up on the horizon. Many bands of horses were now in motion. They streaked to and fro across lighter places in the dust cloud. Pan wanted to stay out in the clear, so that he could see distinctly, but he was already behind his comrades. No horses were running up the wash. So he worked over toward where he had last observed his father, and gave up any attempt at further orderly driving.

It was plain that his comrades had soon broken the line. Probably in such a case, where so many horses were running, it was not possible to keep a uniform front. But Pan thought they could have done better. He saw strings of horses passing him to the left. No doubt the main solid mass was now on a stampede toward the south.

Pan let stragglers and small bunches go by him. There were, however, no large bands of horses running back, at least that he could see. He rode to and fro at a fast clip across this dust-clouded basin, heading what horses happened to come near him. Once he thought he saw a rider on a white mount. Then he decided he was mistaken, for none of Blinky's horses was white.

After a long patrol in the dust and heat of that valley flat, Pan emerged, it seemed, into clearer atmosphere. He was working up. Horses were everywhere, and it was ridiculous to try to drive all that he encountered. At length there was none running back. All were heading across, to and fro, or down the valley. And when Pan reached the long ascent of that bowl, he saw a magnificent spectacle.

A long black mass of horses was sweeping onward toward the gateway to the corrals, and to the fence. Dust columns, like smoke, curled up from behind them, and swung low on the breeze. Pan saw riders behind them, and to the left. He had perhaps been the only one to go through that valley bowl. The many bands of horses, now converged into one great herd, had no doubt crossed it. They were fully four miles distant. Pan saw his opportunity to cut across and down to the right toward where the fence met the wash. If the horses swerved, as surely some or all of them would do, he could head them off. To that end he gave Sorrel free rein and had a splendid run of several miles to the point halfway between the fence and the wash.

Here, from a high point of ground, he observed the moving pace of dust, and the black wheel-shaped mass of horses sweep down the valley like a storm. The spectacle was worth all the toil and time he had given, even if not one beast was captured. But Pan, with swelling heart and beaming eye, felt assured of greater success than he had hoped for. There were five thousand horses in that band, more by ten times than he had ever before seen driven. They could not all get through that narrow gateway to the corrals. Pan wondered how his few riders could have done so well. Luck! The topography of the valley! The wild horses took the lanes of least resistance, and the level or downhill ground favored a broad direct line toward the fence trap Pan had contrived.

"Looks like Dad and all the rest of them have swung 'round on this side," soliloquized Pan, straining his eyes.

That was good, but Pan could not understand how they had ever accomplished it. Perhaps they had been keen enough to see that the horses would not have to go through the gateway or turn south along the fence.

Pan watched eagerly. Whatever was going to happen must come very soon, as swiftly as those fast wild horses could run another mile. He saw them sweep down on the bluff, and around it, and then begin to spread, to disintegrate. Again dust clouds settled over one place. It was in the apex. What a vortex of furious horses must be there! Pan lost sight of them for some moments. Then out of the yellow curtain streaked black strings, traveling down the fence toward Pan, across the valley, back up the way they had come. Pan let out a stentorian yell of victory. He knew that the action indicated that the horses had poured in a mass into the apex between bluff and fence.

"*Whoopee!*" yelled Pan, to relieve his surcharged emotions. "It's a sure bet we've got a bunch!"

Then he spurred Sorrel to meet the horses fleeing down along the fence. They came toward him in bunches, in lines, stringing for a mile or more along the barrier of cedars.

Pan met them with yells and shouts. Frantic now, the animals wheeled back. But few of them ran up out of the winding shallow ground along which the fence had been cunningly built. He drove them back, up over the slow ascent, toward the dusty swarm of horses that ran helter-skelter under the dust haze.

Suddenly Pan espied a black stallion racing toward him. He remembered the horse. And the desire to capture this individual took strong hold upon him. The advantage lay all with Pan. So he held back.

At the most favorable moment Pan spurred Sorrel to inter-

126

cept the stallion. But the black, maddened with terror and instinct with rage, would not swerve out of Pan's way. On he came, swift as the wind, lean black head out, mane flying, a wild creature at once beautiful and fearful. Pan had to jerk Sorrel out of his way. Then, having the black between himself and the fence, Pan turned Sorrel loose. The race began—with Pan still holding the advantage. It did not, however, last long that way. The black ran away from Pan. He wanted to shoot but thought it best not to use his last shells. What a stride! He was a big horse, too, ragged, rangy, with action and power that delighted Pan.

Knowing he could not catch the black, Pan cut across toward the wash. Then the stallion, seeing the yawning gulf ahead, turned toward the fence, and quickening that marvelous stride he made a magnificent leap right at the top of the obstruction. He cleared the heavy wood and crashed through the branches to freedom.

"You black son-of-a-gun!" Pan yelled in sheer admiration, and, halting the sorrel, he watched the stallion disappear.

Dust-begrimed and wet, Pan once more headed toward the goal. His horse was tired, and so was he. Far as he could view in a fan-shaped spread, wild horses were running back up the valley. Pan estimated he saw thousands, but there were no heavy black masses, no sweeping storm-like clouds of horses, such as had borne down on that corner of the valley.

He was weary, but he could have sung for very joy. Happily his thoughts reverted to Lucy and the future. He would pick out a couple of beautiful ponies for her and break them gently. He could find some swift, sturdy horses for himself. Then, as many thousands of times, he thought of his first horse, Curly. None could ever take his place. But how he would have loved to own the black stallion.

"I'm just as glad, though he got away," mused Pan.

The afternoon was half gone and hazy, owing to the drifting clouds of dust that had risen from the valley. As Pan neared the end of the fence, which was still a goodly distance from the gateway, he was surprised that he did not see any horses or men. The wide brush gates had been closed. Beyond them and over the bluff he saw clouds of dust, like smoke, rising lazily, as if just stirred.

"Horses in the corrals!" he exclaimed. "I'll bet they're full. . . . Now comes the problem! But we could hold a thousand head there for a week . . . maybe ten days. There's water and grass. Reckon, though, I'll see tomorrow."

He would have hurried on but for the fact that Sorrel had begun to limp. Pan remembered going over a steep soft bank where the horse had stumbled. Dismounting, Pan walked the rest of the way to the bluff, beginning to think it strange he did not see or hear any of his comrades. No doubt they were back reveling in the corrals full of wild horses.

"It's been a great day. If only I could get word to Lucy!"

Pan opened the small gate and led Sorrel into the lane. Still he did not see anything of the men. He did hear, however, a snorting, trampling of many horses, over in the direction of the farther corral.

At the end of the bluff, where the line of slope curved in deep, Pan suddenly saw a number of saddled horses, without riders.

With a violent start he halted.

There were men, strange men, standing in groups, lounging on the rocks, sitting down, all as if waiting.

A little to the left of these Pan's lightning-swift gaze took in another group. His men! Not lounging, not conversing, but aloof from each other, lax and abject, or strung motionless!

Bewildered, shocked, Pan swept his eyes back upon the strangers.

"Hardman! Purcell!" he gasped, starting back as if struck.

Then his mind leaped to conclusions. He did not need to see Blinky approach him with hard, sullen face. Hardman and his outfit had timed the wild horse drive. No doubt they had participated in it, and meant to profit by that, or, worse, they meant to claim the drive, and by superior numbers force that issue.

Such a terrible fury possessed Pan that he burned and shook all over. He dropped his bridle and made a dragging step to meet Blinky. But so great was his emotion that he had no physical control. He waited. After that bursting of his heart, he slowly changed. This then was the strange untoward thing that had haunted him. All the time fate had held this horrible crisis in abeyance, waiting to crush at the last moment this marvelous good fortune. An icy misery convulsed him for a moment. But that could not exist in the white heat of his wrath.

"Blink . . . Blink," whispered Pan hoarsely, "it's come, that hunch we feared, but wouldn't believe!"

"I . . . I couldn't hev told you," Blinky replied just as hoarsely. "An' it couldn't be worse!"

"Blink . . . then we made a good haul?"

"Cowboy, nobody ever heard of such a haul. We could moonshine wild hosses fer a hundred years an' never ketch as many."

"How . . . many?" Pan queried sharply, his voice breaking clear.

"I say fifteen hundred haid. Your dad, who's about crazy,

reckons two thousand. An' the other fellars come in between."

"Fifteen hundred horses!" ejaculated Pan intensely. "Heavens, but it's great!"

"Pan, I wish we hadn't ketched any," Blinky declared in a hard, fierce voice.

That brought Pan back to earth.

"What's their game?" he asked swiftly, indicating the watching, whispering group.

"I had only a few words with Hardman. Your dad went out of his haid. Reckon he'd have done fer Hardman with his bare hands, if Purcell hadn't knocked him down with the barrel of a gun."

Again there was a violent leap of Pan's blood.

"Blink, did that big brute . . . ?" Pan asked hoarsely, suddenly breaking off.

"He shore did. Your dad's got a nasty knock over the eye. No, I hadn't any chance to talk to Hardman. But his game's as plain as that big nose of his."

"Well, what is it?" snapped Pan.

"Shore he'll grab our hosses, or most of them," returned Blinky.

"You mean straight horse stealing?"

"Shore. But the worst of it is Hardman's outfit helped make the drive."

"No!"

"You bet they did. Thet's what galls me. Either they was layin' fer the day or just happened to ride up on us, an' figgered it out. Mebbe thet's where MacNew comes in."

"Blink, I don't believe he's double-crossed us," Pan declared stoutly. "But we'll find out. So you think Hardman will claim most of our horses, or take them all?"

"I shore do."

"Blink, if he gets *one* of our horses, it'll be over my dead body. You fellows sure showed yellow clear through . . . to let them ride in here without a fight."

Blinky cried out an oath as if stung. "What do you think? There wasn't one of us thet had a single load left fer our guns. We played their game. Wasted a lot of shells on them damn' broomies! So how could we fight?"

"A-huh," groaned Pan, appalled at the fatality of the whole incident. With that he whirled on his heel and strode forward toward where Hardman, Purcell, and another man stood apart from the lounging riders.

Slowly Blinky followed in Pan's footsteps, and then MacNew left the group in the shade of the wall, and shuffled out into the sunlight.

As Pan approached, Purcell swung around square with his hands low, a significant posture. Hardman evinced signs of extreme nervous tension. The third man walked apart from them. All the others abandoned their lounging attitude.

"Hardman, what's your game?" Pan queried bluntly as he halted.

Hardman braced himself.

"Game?" he parried gruffly. "There's no game about drivin' a million wild horses through the dust. It was work."

"Don't try to twist words with me," replied Pan fiercely. "What's your game?"

"We made the drive, Smith," returned Hardman. "You'd never made it without us. An' that gives us the biggest share. Say two-thirds, an' I'll buy your third at ten dollars a head."

"Hardman, that's a rotten deal," burst out Pan. "Haven't you any sense? We planned this trap. We worked like dogs. And we made the drive. You might account for more horses trapped, but no difference. You had no business here."

"Wal, if I've got the hosses, I don't care what *you* say," Hardman retorted, finding bravado as the interview progressed.

It was no use trying to appeal to any sense of fairness in this man. Pan saw that, and his passionate eloquence died in his throat. Coldly he eyed Hardman, and then the greasy dust-caked face of Purcell. He could catch only the steely speculation in Purcell's eyes.

Meanwhile, Blinky had come up beside Pan, and a moment later MacNew. Their actions, especially MacNew's, were not to be misunderstood. The situation became more tense. Hardman suddenly showed the strain.

Pan's demeanor, however, might have been deceiving, except to the keenest of men, long versed in such encounters.

"Jard Hardman, you're a low-down horse thief," Pan said deliberately.

The taunt, thrown in Hardman's face, added to the tension of the moment. He recognized at last something beyond his power to change or stop.

"Smith, reckon you've cause for temper," he said huskily. "I'll take half the hosses . . . an' buy your half."

"No! Not one broomtail do you get," returned Pan in a voice that cut. "Look out, Hardman! I can prove you hatched up this deal to rob me."

"How, I'd like to know?" blustered the rancher, relaxing again.

"MacNew can prove it."

"Who's he?"

"Hurd here. His real name is MacNew. You hired him to get in with me . . . to keep you posted on my movements."

Again Hardman showed his kind of fiber under extreme

provocation: "Yes, I hired him . . . an' he's double-crossed you as well as me."

"Did he? Well, now *you* prove that," flashed Pan, who had read the furious falseness of the man.

"Purcell here," Hardman replied hoarsely. "He's been camped below. Hurd met him at night . . . kept him posted on your work. Then, when all was ready for the drive, Purcell sent for me."

"Hardman, you're a liar!" MacNew roared sonorously. If ever Pan heard menace in a voice, it was then. "Take it back!" went on the outlaw. "Square me with Panhandle Smith!"

"Mac, he doesn't have to square you. Anyone could see he's a liar!" called Pan derisively.

"Hurd, I . . . I'll have you shot . . . I'll shoot you myself!" Hardman burst out, wresting his arm toward his hip.

A thundering report close beside Pan almost deafened him. Hardman uttered a loud gasp. Then like a flung sack he fell heavily.

"Thar, Jard Hardman," declared the outlaw. "I had one bullet left." And he threw his empty gun with violence at the prostrate body.

Purcell's long taut body jerked into swift action. His gun spurted red as it leaped out. Pan, quick as he drew and shot, was too late to save MacNew. Both men fell without a cry.

"Blink, grab their guns!" Pan yelled piercingly, and, leaping over the bodies, he confronted the stricken group of men with leveled weapon.

"Hands up! Quick!" he ordered fiercely.

His swiftness, his tremendous passion, had shocked Hardman's men. Up went their hands.

Then Blinky ran in with a gun in each hand, and his wild

aspect most powerfully supplemented Pan's furious menace.

"Fork them hosses!" yelled Blinky with a furious oath. Death for more of them quivered in the balance. As one man Hardman's riders rushed to mount their horses. Several did not wait for further orders, but plunged away down the lane toward the outlet.

Chapter Fourteen

The two horses left, belonging to Hardman and Purcell, neighed loudly at being left behind, and pulled on their halters.

Pan's quick eye caught sight of a rifle in a sheath on one of the saddles. He ran to get it. Blinky, observing Pan's act, repeated it with the other horse.

Pan hurriedly sheathed his gun and, with the rifle in hand, ran back to the overhanging bluff, where he began to climb through the brush. Fierce action was necessary to him then. When he looked out upon the valley, he espied Hardman's outfit two miles down the slope, beyond the cedar fence. They had ridden hard to the cedars.

Then a reaction set in upon Pan. He crawled into the shade of some brush and stretched out, letting his tight muscles relax. The terrible something released its hold on mind and heart. He was sick. He fought himself until the spasm passed.

When he got back to his men, it took some effort for Pan to approach his father.

"How are you, Dad?" he asked with constraint.

"Little shaky . . . I . . . guess . . . Son," came the husky reply. But Bill Smith got up and removed his hand from the wound on his forehead.

"Nasty bump, Dad. I'll bet you'll have a headache. Go to

camp and bathe it in cold water. Then get Juan to bandage it."

"All right," replied his father. He forced himself to look up at Pan. His eyes were warming out of deep strange shadows of pain, of horror. "Son, I . . . I was kind of dazed when . . . when you . . . the fight come off. . . . I heard the shots, but I didn't see. . . . Was it you who . . . who killed Jard Hardman?"

"No, Dad," Pan replied, placing a steady hand on his father's shoulder. "MacNew shot him. Hardman accused Mac of double-crossing me. Mac called him. I think Hardman tried to draw. But Mac killed him. . . . I got Purcell too late to save Mac."

The trapped wild horses, cracking their hoofs and whistling in the huge corrals, did not at the moment attract Pan, or wean him away from the deep unsettled condition of mind. As he passed the corral on the way to the camp, the horses moved with a trampling roar. The sound helped him toward gaining a hold on his normal self.

The hour now was near sunset, and the heat of day had passed. A cool light breeze made a soft low sound in the trees.

Pan found his father sitting with bandaged head beside the campfire, and apparently recovering somewhat.

While they were talking, Gus Hans and Charley Brown returned to camp. They were leading the horses that had been ridden by Hardman and Purcell.

"Turn them loose, boys," directed Pan, to whom they looked for instructions.

Presently Gus handed Pan a heavy wallet and a huge roll of greenbacks.

"Found the wallet on Purcell an' the roll on Hardman," said Gus.

"But what'll I do with all this?" Pan queried blankly.

"Pard, you seem to forget Hardman owed your Dad money."

"Dad, you never told me how much Hardman did you out of," said Pan.

"Ten thousand in cash, an' Lord only knows how many cattle."

"So much! I'd imagined . . . say, Dad, will you take this money?"

"Yes, if it's honest an' regular for me to do so," Bill Smith replied stoutly.

"Regular? There's no law in Marco. We've got to make our own laws. Let it be a matter of conscience. Boys, this man Hardman ruined my father. I heard that from a reliable source at Littletown before I ever got here. Don't you think it honest for Dad to take this money?"

"Shore, it's more than thet," replied Blinky. "I'd call it justice. If you turned thet money over to the law in Marco, it'd go to Matthews. An' you can bet your socks he'd keep it."

The consensus of opinion did not differ materially from Blinky's.

"Dad, it's a long trail that has no turning," Pan said, tossing both wallet and roll to his father. "Here's to your new ranch in Arizona!"

Lying Juan soon called them to supper. It was not the usual cheery meal. The sudden terrible catastrophe of the day did not quickly release its somber grip.

Afterward, Pan lay awake in his blankets. He could not sleep. He could not keep his eyes shut. What question shone down in the pitiless stars? Something strange and inscrutable weighed upon him. Was it a new-born conscience, stirred by his return to his mother, by his love for Lucy? He seemed to be haunted. Reason told him that it was well he had come to fight for his father. He could not be blamed for the machinations of evil men. He suffered no regret, no remorse. Yet there was something that he could not understand. It was a physical sensation that gave him a chill creeping of his flesh. It was also a spiritual shrinking, a withdrawing from what he knew not.

Other times he had felt the encroachment of this insidious thing, but vague and raw. Whisky had been a cure. But he could not yield to that. Not now, with Lucy's face like a wraith floating in the starlight! He was conscious of love, home, children. Yet beautiful as was that dream, it could not be realized in these days without the deadly spirit and violence to which he had just answered. That was the bitter anomaly.

Next morning, in the sweet cedar-tanged air and the rosy-gold of the sunrise, Pan was himself again, keen for the day. His father approached briskly, his face shining. He was a different man.

"Blinky, trapping these wild horses and handling them are two different things," remarked Pan thoughtfully. "Reckon I'll have to pass the buck to you."

"Wal, pard, I'm shore there. We'll chase all the hosses into the big corral. Then we'll pick out one at a time, an', if we cain't rope him without scarin' the bunch too bad, we'll chase him into the small corral."

Gus and Brown brought in the saddle horses, and soon the men were riding down to the corrals. Upon their entrance to the first and smaller corral a string of lean, ragged, wild-eyed mustangs trooped with a roar back into the larger corral.

It was a magnificent sight. Whether or not there was much fine stock among them or even any, the fact remained that hundreds of wild horses together in one drove, captive and knowing it, were collected in this great trap, and the intense

138

vitality of them, the vivid coloring, the beautiful action of many, and the statuesque immobility of the majority, were thrillingly all-satisfying to the hearts of the captors.

"Regular lot of broomtails!" Blinky yelled to Pan. "Ain't seen any yet I'd give two bits fer."

But Pan inclined to the opinion that among so many there were surely a few fine animals. And so it proved. Pan's first choice was a blue roan, a rare combination of color, build, and speed. He pointed her out to Blinky and Gus, and the chase began. They headed the roan off, hedged her in a triangle, cut her out from the other horses, and toward the open gate. She bolted through it.

Gus made a beautiful throw with his lasso, a whirling wide loop that seemed to shoot perpendicularly across in front of her. She ran into it, and the violent check brought her down. Blinky was almost waiting to kneel on her head. And Gus, leaping off, hobbled her front feet.

Warming to the work, they went back among the circling animals. By noon they had ten hobbled in the open pasture. Two of these were Pan's. He had been hard to please.

"Wal, we'll rest the hosses an' go get some chuck," suggested Blinky.

Early afternoon found them again hard at their task. The wild horses had not only grown tired from trooping around the corral, but also somewhat used to the riders.

"Let's call it off!" Blinky finally shouted. "I'm satisfied, if you are."

"Aw, just one more, pard," implored Pan. "I've had my eye on a little bay mare with four white socks. She's got a V Bar brand, and she's not so wild."

In the end, they got Little Bay—as Pan had already named her—into the roping corral, along with two other horses that ran in with her. There Pan chased her into a corner and threw a noose round her neck. She reared and snorted, but did not bolt.

Pan was enraptured with the beauty of the little bay. He had no way to guess how long she had been free, but he concluded not a great while, because she was not so wild.

"Pard, this little bay is fer your gurl, huh?" queried Blinky.

"You guessed right, Blink," answered Pan. "Little Bay . . . that's her name."

"Wal, now you got thet off your chest, s'pose you climb on your hoss an' look heah," added Blinky.

The tone of his voice, the way he pointed over the cedar fence to the slope, caused Pan to leap into his saddle. In a moment his sweeping gaze caught horsemen and pack animals zigzagging down the trail.

"If it's Hardman's outfit, they're comin' back with nerve," Blinky said. "But I never figgered they'd come."

Pan cursed under his breath. In a flash he was hard and stern.

"Ride, Blink," he replied briefly.

They made their way back to camp with eyes ever on the zigzag trail, where, in openings among the cedars, the horsemen could be occasionally seen.

"Pard, are you goin' to let them ride right into camp?" Blinky queried.

"I guess not," Pan replied bluntly. "Rifle shot is near enough."

After a long interval fraught with anxiety and suspense, during which the horsemen approached steadily, growing more distinct, Blinky burst out: "Fellars, shore as you're born, it's Wiggett!"

"The horse dealer from Saint Louis!" ejaculated Pan in tremendous relief.

"It's Wiggett, Son," corroborated Pan's father. "I met him

once. He's a broad heavy man with a thin gray chin beard."

The approaching horseman halted within earshot.

"Hi, there, camp!" called the leader, whose appearance tallied with Smith's description.

"Hello," replied Pan striding out.

"Who's boss here?"

"Reckon I am."

"My name's Wiggett," replied the other.

"All right, Mister Wiggett," Pan returned. "What's your business?"

"Friendly. I want to talk horses."

"Come on up, then."

Whereupon the group of horsemen advanced. The foremost was a large man, rather florid, with deep-set eyes and scant gray beard.

"Are you the younger Smith?" he asked, rather nervously eyeing Pan.

"Yes, sir."

"And you're in charge here?"

Pan nodded shortly.

"Word come to me this morning that you'd trapped a large number of horses," went on Wiggett. "I see that's a fact. It's a wonderful sight. Of course, you expect to make a deal for them?"

"Yes. No trading. No percentage. I want cash. They're a shade better stock than you've been buying around Marco."

"How many?"

"We disagree as to numbers. But I say close to fifteen hundred head."

"Good Lord!" boomed the big man. "It's a haul, indeed. I'll give you our regular price, twelve-fifty, delivered in Marco."

"No, thanks," replied Pan.

"Thirteen."

Pan shook his head. "I'll sell for ten dollars a head, cash, and count and deliver them here tomorrow."

"Sold!" snapped out Wiggett.

"Thank you . . . Mister Wiggett," replied Pan, suddenly rather halting in speech. "That'll suit us."

"May we pitch camp here?"

"Sure. Get down and come in."

Pan had to get away then for a while from his father and the exuberant Blinky. How could they forget the dead men over there, still unburied? Pan had read in Wiggett's look and speech and in the faces of his men that they had been told of the killing, and surely to the discredit of Pan and his followers. Pan vowed he would put Wiggett in possession of the facts.

Later he mingled again with the men around the campfire. Some of the restraint had disappeared, at least in regard to Wiggett and his men toward everybody except Pan. At an opportune moment he confronted the horse buyer.

"How'd you learn about this drive of ours?" he asked briefly.

"Hardman's men rode into Marco this morning," Wiggett replied coldly.

"A-huh. And they told a cock-and-bull story about what happened out here?"

"It placed you in a bad light, young man."

"I reckon. Well, if you or any of your outfit or anybody else calls me a horse thief, he wants to go for his gun. Do you understand that?"

"It's pretty plain English," Wiggett replied manifestly concerned.

"And here's some more. Jard Hardman *was* a horse thief," went on Pan, in rising passion. "He hired men to steal for him. And, by heaven, he wasn't half as white as the outlaw who killed him!"

"Outlaw? I declare . . . we . . . I . . . do you mean you're an . . . ?" Wiggett floundered. "We understood you killed Hardman."

"No!" Blinky shouted, aflame with fury. "We was all there. We saw. . . ."

"Wiggett, you listen to me first," broke in Pan, with no lessening of his intensity. Then he told in stern brevity the true details of that triple killing. After concluding, with white face and sharp gesture, he indicated to his men that they were to corroborate his statement.

"Mister Wiggett, it's God's truth," Pan's father spoke up earnestly. "It was just retribution. Hardman robbed me years ago."

Gus stepped forward without any show of excitement.

"If you need evidence other than our word, it's easy to find," he said. "MacNew's gun was not the same caliber as Pan's. An' as the bullet thet killed Hardman is still in his body, it can be found."

"Gentlemen, that isn't necessary," Wiggett replied hastily, with a shudder. "Not for me. But my men can substantiate it. That might sound well in Marco. For I believe your young leader . . . Panhandle Smith, they call him . . . is not so black as he has been painted."

Chapter Fifteen

The following morning, while Pan was away for a few hours, deer hunting, Wiggett's men, accompanied by Blinky, attended to the gruesome detail of burying the dead men.

Upon Pan's return he learned of this and experienced relief that Wiggett had taken the responsibility.

Wiggett had all his men, except the one he had sent back to Marco, engaged in counting the captured wild horses. It was a difficult task.

"Anxious to get back to Marco?" Wiggett queried not unkindly, as he saw Pan's restlessness.

"Yes, I am, now the job's done."

"Well, I wouldn't be in any hurry, if I were you," said the horse dealer bluntly.

"What do you mean?" queried Pan.

"Young Hardman is to be reckoned with."

"Bah!" burst out Pan, in a scorn that was rude although he meant it for Hardman. "What do I care for him?"

"Excuse me, I would not presume to advise you," Wiggett returned stiffly.

"Aw, beg your pardon, Mister Wiggett," apologized Pan. "I know you mean well. And I sure thank you."

Wiggett did not answer, but he took something from his vest pocket. It was a lead bullet, slightly flattened.

"Let me see your gun?" he asked.

Pan handed the weapon to him, butt first. Wiggett took it gingerly, and tried to fit the bullet in a chamber of the cylinder, and then in the barrel. It was too large to go in.

"This is the bullet that killed Hardman," Wiggett said gravely. "It was never fired from your gun. I shall take pains to make this evident in Marco."

"I don't know that it matters, but I'm sure much obliged," returned Pan.

"Well, I'll do it anyhow. I've been fooled by Hardman, and cheated, too. That's why I broke with him."

According to figures that the counters agreed upon, there were fourteen hundred and eighty-six horses in the trap.

Wiggett paid cash upon the spot. Pan doubled the wages of those who had been hired. Then he divided what was left with Blinky.

"But, pard, it's too much," appealed Blinky. "This was your drive."

"Yes, and it was your outfit," returned Pan. "You furnished the packs, horses, and I furnished the execution. Looks like a square deal, share and share alike."

"All right, pard," Blinky replied, swallowing hard. "If you reckon thet way. . . . But will you keep this heah roll for me . . . I'll go on a tear."

"Blink, you're not going to drink, unless in that one deal I hinted about," Pan said with meaning. "Hope we can avoid it."

"Aw, we're turnin' over a new leaf, huh?" queried the cowboy.

"You are, Blink," Pan replied with a frank, serious smile. "You've been terrible bad."

"Who said so?" retorted Blinky aggrievedly.

"I heard it at the Yellow Mine."

That name and the implication conveyed by Pan made

Blinky drop his head. But his somber shame quickly fled.

"Wal, pard, I'll stay sober as long as you. Shake on it."

Pan made his plans to leave next morning as early as the wild horses they had hobbled could be gotten into shape to travel. Wiggett expected the riders he had sent for to arrive before noon the next day; it was his opinion that he would have all the horses he had purchased out of there in a week. Pan and Blinky did not share this opinion.

In the gray of dawn when the kindling east had begun to dwarf the glory of the morning star, the cowboys drove all the hobbled horses into the smaller corral. There they roped off a corner, and hung a white tarpaulin over the rope. This was an improvised second corral where they would put the horses, one by one, as they tied up one hoof of each animal.

It took two hours of exceedingly strenuous labor to tie up all the wild horses. Each horse had presented a new fight. Then came the quick job of packing their outfits. At nine o'clock they were ready for the momentous twenty-five mile drive to Marco, with Snyder's pasture as the stopping place for the night.

As Pan rode up the ridge leading out of the valley, he turned to have a last look at this memorable place. To his amaze and delight he saw almost as many wild horses as before the drive.

The parade, as Blinky had called it, made only a few miles an hour, and sometimes this advance was not wholly in the right direction. When at about ten o'clock at night Blinky espied through the gloom landmarks that indicated Snyder's pasture, it was none too soon for Pan.

The weary riders unpacked the outfit, took a long deep drink of the cold water, and, unrolling their tarps, went supperless to bed. Pan's eyes closed as if with glue, and his thoughts wavered, faded.

Pan's father was the first to get up, but already the sun was before him.

"Pile out!" he yelled. "It's Siccane, Arizona, or bust!"

"Wal, our hosses are heah," Blinky said cheerfully. "Reckon I was afraid they'd jump the fence. I'm gamblin' in three hours we'll have them in your dad's corral."

"Say, Blink, do we take this road on our way south to Siccane?"

"Yep. It's the only road."

"Then, by golly, we can leave our new horses here!" Pan exclaimed gladly.

"Wal, I'll be god-darned. Where's my haid? Shore we can. But we cain't leave these hosses unguarded."

"I'll stay," said Gus. "It's a good idee. An' I reckon I'd like a job with you, far as Siccane anyway."

"You've got it, and after we reach Siccane, too," replied Pan quickly.

As he rode out that morning on the sorrel, to face north on the road to Marco, he found it hard to contain himself. This hour was the very first in which he could let himself think of the glorious fulfillment of his dream.

Almost he loved this wild and rugged land. The sky was as blue as the inside of a columbine; a rich and beautiful light of gold gilded the wall of rock that boldly cropped out of the mountainside; and the wide, sweeping expanse of sage lost itself in a deep purple horizon. The air was sweet, intoxicating.

While he saw and felt all this, his mind scintillated with thoughts of Lucy Blake. He would see her presently, have the joy of surprising her into betrayal of love.

147

Dreaming thus, Pan rode along without being aware of the time or distance.

"Hey, pard!" Blinky called in loud banter. "Are you goin' to ride past where your gurl lives?"

With a violent start Pan wheeled his horse. He saw that he had, indeed, ridden beyond the entrance to a farm, which upon second look he recognized.

"I'm loco, all right," he replied.

Bill Smith smiled.

Through gate and lane they galloped, on to the corral, and around that to the barn. This was only a short distance from the house. Pan leaped from his horse and ran.

The door was shut. Stealthily he tiptoed across the porch to knock. No answer! He tried the door. Locked! A quiver ran through him.

"Strange," he muttered, "not home this early."

He peered through the window, to see on floor and table ample evidence of recent packing. Perhaps his mother and Lucy had gone into Marco to purchase necessities.

"But . . . didn't I tell Lucy not to go?" he queried in bewilderment.

Resolutely he cast out doubtful speculations. There could hardly be anything wrong. Hurriedly he returned to the barn.

"Wal, I'll tell you," Blinky was holding forth blandly to Bill Smith, "this heah grubbin' around without a home an' a woman ain't no good. I'm shore through. I'm goin'. . . ."

"Nobody home," interrupted Pan. "I've got to find Lucy *pronto*. But where?"

With a single step he reached his stirrup and swung into his saddle.

"Pan, Lucy an' the wife will be in one of the stores," Bill Smith said. "Don't worry about them. Why, they're doing all our buyin'."

"I tell you I don't like it," snapped Pan. "It's not what I think, but what I feel. All the same, wherever they are it doesn't change our plans. I'll sure find them, and tell them we're packing to leave *pronto*."

Blinky joined him, leaving Bill Smith behind. They rode rapidly until they reached the outskirts of town, when Blinky called Pan to a halt.

"Reckon you'd better not ride through the main street," he said significantly.

They tied their horses behind a clump of trees between two deserted shacks. They passed a vacant lot on one side of the street and framed tents on the other. Presently they could see down the whole of the main street. Pan fancied there was more activity than usual. That might have been owing to the fact that both the incoming and outgoing stages were visible far up at the end of the street.

Pan strained his eyes at people near and far, seeking some sign of Lucy. Soon he would reach the first store. But before he got there, he saw his mother emerge, dragging Bobby. Then Alice followed. Both she and her mother were carrying bundles. Pan's heart made ready for a greater leap—in anticipation of Lucy's appearance. But she did not come.

Pan, striding ahead of Blinky, saw his mother turn white and reel as if about to faint. Pan got to her in time.

"Mother . . . why, Mother," he cried, in mingled gladness and distress, "it's me! I'm all right."

His mother clung to him with hands like steel. "Pan! Pan! Oh, thank God! They told us you'd been shot."

"Me? Well, I guess not. I'm better than ever, and full of good news," Pan went on hurriedly. "Brace up, Mother. We've got a lot to do. Where's Lucy?"

His mother wheeled to point up the street.

"Lucy! There . . . in that stage . . . leaving Marco!"

Something terrible seemed to crash inside Pan. Catastrophe! It was here.

"Mother, go home at once," he said swiftly. "Tell Dad to rush buying the wagons. You and Alice pack. We shake the dust of this town. Don't worry. Lucy will leave with us!"

Then Pan broke into long springy strides, almost a run. Indeed, Blinky had to run to keep up with him.

People rushed into the street to get out of the way of the cowboys. Booted men on the porch of the Yellow Mine stamped noisily as they trooped to get inside. Voices of alarm and mirth rang out.

They reached the end of the street, and across the wide square stood the outgoing stage, before the express office. There was no driver on the front seat. Jones, the agent, was emerging from the office with mailbags.

"Slow up, pard," whispered Blinky.

Pan did as he was advised, although his stride still retained speed. Impossible to go slowly. There were passengers in the stagecoach. When Pan reached the middle of the street, he saw a gleam of golden hair that he knew. Lucy! Her back was turned to him. And as he recognized her, realized he had found her, there burst thundering clamor of questioning voices in his mind.

A few more strides took him around the stage. Men backed away from him. The door was open.

"Lucy!" he cried. "What does this mean? Where are you going?"

She could not speak. But under her pallor the red of shame began to burn. Mutely he gazed at the girl as her head slowly sank. Then he asked hoarsely: "What's it mean?"

"Pard, take a peep 'round heah," drawled Blinky in slow cool speech.

Pan wheeled. He had the shock of his life. He received it

before his whirling thoughts recorded the reason. It was as if he had to look twice. Dick Hardman! Fashionably and wonderfully attired! Pan got no further than sight of the frock coat, elaborate vest, flowing tie, and high hat. Then for a second he went blind.

When the red film cleared, he saw Hardman pass him, saw the pallor of his cheek, the quivering of muscle.

He got one foot on the stage step when Pan found release for his voice.

"Hardman!"

That halted the youth, as if it had been a rope, but he never turned his head.

Pan leaped at Hardman and spun him round.

"Where are you going?"

"Frisco, if it's . . . any of your business," muttered Hardman.

"Looks like I'll make it my business," Pan returned menacingly. He could not be himself here. The shock had been too great. His mind seemed stultified. "Hardman . . . do you mean . . . do you think . . . you're taking her away?" Pan queried as if strangling.

"Ha!" Hardman returned with an upfling of head, arrogant, vain for all his fear. "I know it. She's my wife!"

Chapter Sixteen

Destruction, death itself seemed to overthrow Panhandle Smith's intensity of life. He reeled on his feet. For a moment all seemed opaque, with blurred images. There was a *crash, crash, crash* of something beating at his ears.

How long this terrible oblivion possessed Pan he did not know. But at Hardman's move to enter the stage, he came back a million times more alive than ever he had been—possessed of devils.

With one powerful lunge he jerked Hardman back and flung him sprawling into the dust.

"There! Once more!" Pan cried pantingly. "Remember . . . the schoolhouse? That fight over Lucy Blake! Curse your skunk soul! Get up, if you've got a gun!"

Hardman leaned on his hand. His high hat had rolled away. His broadcloth suit was covered with dust. But he did not note these details of his abasement. Like a craven thing fascinated by a snake, he had his starting eyes fixed upon Pan, and his face was something no man could bear to see.

"Get up . . . if you've got a gun!" ordered Pan.

"I've no . . . gun . . . ," he replied in husky accents.

"Talk, then. Maybe I can keep from killing you."

"For heaven's sake . . . don't shoot me. I'll tell you anything."

"Hardman, you say you . . . you married my . . . this girl?"

rasped out Pan, choking over his words as if they were poison, unable to speak of Lucy as he had thought of her all his life.

"Yes . . . I married her."

"Who married you?"

"A parson from Salt Lake. Matthews got him here."

"A-huh! Matthews. How did you force her?"

"I swear she was willing," went on Hardman. "Her father wanted her to."

"What? Jem Blake left here for Arizona. I sent him away."

"But he never went . . . I . . . I mean he got caught . . . put in jail again. Matthews sent for the officers. They came. And they said they'd put Blake away for ten years. But I got him off. Then Lucy was willing to marry me . . . and she did. There's no help for it now. Too late."

"Liar!" hissed Pan. "You frightened her . . . tortured her."

"No, I didn't do anything. It was her father. He persuaded her."

"Drove her, you mean. And you paid him. Admit it or I'll. . . ." Pan's move was threatening.

"Yes . . . yes, I did," Hardman jerked out in hoarser lower voice. Something about his lifelong foe appalled him. He was abject. No confession of his guilt was needed.

"Go get yourself a gun. You'll have to kill me before you start out on your honeymoon. Reckon I think you're going to hell. Get up. . . . Go get yourself a gun."

Hardman staggered to his feet, brushing the dirt from his person while he gazed strickenly at Pan.

"I can't fight you," he said. "You won't murder me in cold blood. Smith, I'm Lucy's husband. . . . She's my wife."

"And what is Louise Melliss?" whipped out Pan. "What does she say about your marriage? You ruined her. You brought her here to Marco. You tired of her. You abandoned her to that hellhole owned by your father. He got his just desserts, and you'll get yours."

Hardman had no answer. Like a dog under the lash he cringed at Pan's words.

"Get out of my sight!" cried Pan. "And remember the next time I see you I'll begin to shoot."

Pan struck him, shoved him out into the street. Hardman staggered on, forgetting his high hat that lay in the dust. He got to going faster until he broke into an uneven half run. He kept to the middle of the street until he reached the Yellow Mine where he ran up the steps and disappeared.

Pan backed slowly, step by step. He was coming out of his clamped obsession. His movement was now that of a man gripped by terror. In reality Pan could have faced any peril, any horror, any physical rending of flesh far more easily than this girl who had ruined him.

She had left the stage, and she stood alone. She spoke his name. In the single low word he divined fear. How long had she been that dog's wife? When had she married him? Yesterday, or the day before . . . a week, what did it matter?

"You . . . you!" he burst out helplessly, in the grip of deadly hate and agony. He hated her then—hated her beauty—and the betrayal of her fear for him. What was life to him now? Oh, the insupportable bitterness!

"Go back to my mother," he ordered harshly, and averted his face.

Then he seemed to forget her. He saw Blinky close to him, deeply shaken, yet composed and grim. He heard the movement of many feet, the stamping of hoofs.

"All aboard for Salt Lake!" called the stage driver. Jones, the agent, passed Pan with more mailbags. The strain all about him had broken.

"Pard," he said, laying a hand on Blinky. "Go with her . . .

154

take her to my mother. . . . And leave me alone."

"No," Blinky replied sullenly. "You forget this heah is my deal, too. There's Louise. . . . An' Lucy took her bag an' hurried away. There she's runnin' past the Yellow Mine."

"Blink, did she hear what I said to Hardman about Louise?" Pan asked bitterly.

"Reckon not. Lucy'd keeled over about then. I shoulda kept my eye on her. An' I tell you, pard. . . ."

"Never mind," interrupted Pan. "What's the difference. Whisky! Let's get a drink. It's whisky I want."

"Shore. I told you that a while back. Come on, pard!"

They crossed to the corner saloon, a low dive kept by a Chinaman and frequented by Mexicans and Indians. These poured out pell-mell as the cowboys jangled up to the bar. Jard Hardman's outfit coming to town had prepared the way for this.

"Howdy," was Blinky's greeting to the black bottle that was thumped upon the counter. "You look mighty natural. Heah's to Panhandle Smith!"

Panhandle drank. The fiery liquor burned as it cooled. It inflamed, but did not intoxicate.

Chapter Seventeen

The afternoon had waned. Matthews lay dead in the street. He lay in front of the Yellow Mine, from which he had been driven by men who would no longer stand the strain. It was there he had confronted Panhandle Smith.

The street was deserted except for that black figure laying face down with a gun in his right hand. His black sombrero lay flat. The wind had blown a high hat down the street until it had stopped near the sombrero. Those who peeped out from behind doors or from windows espied these sinister objects.

Pan had patrolled the street. He had made a house to house canvas, searching for Jem Blake. He had entered every place except the Yellow Mine. That he reserved for the last. But he did not find Blake. He encountered, however, a slight pale man in clerical garb.

"Are you the parson Matthews brought to Marco?" Pan demanded harshly.

"Yes, sir," came the reply.

"Did you marry young Hardman to . . . to . . . ?" Pan could not end the query.

The minister was too dumbfounded to speak, but his affirmative was not necessary.

"Man, you may be innocent of evil intent. But you ruined my . . . girl . . . and me! You've sent me to hell. I ought to kill you."

"Pard, shore we mushn't kill thish heah parson just yet," Blinky drawled thickly. "He'll come in handy."

"A-huh. Right you are, Blinky," returned Pan, with a ghastly pretense of gaiety. "Parson, stay right here till we come for you. Maybe you can make up a little for the wrong you did one girl."

The Yellow Mine stood with glass uplifted and card unplayed.

Pan had entered from the dance hall entrance. Blinky, unsteady on his feet, came in from the street. After a tense moment the poker players went on with their game, and the drinkers emptied their glasses. But voices were low, glances were furtive.

Pan had seen every man there before he had been seen himself. Only one interested him—that was Jem Blake. What to do to this man or with him?—Pan found it hard to decide. Blake had, indeed, fallen low. But Pan gave him the benefit of one doubt—that he had been wholly dominated by Hardman. Yet there was the matter of accepting money for his part in forcing Lucy to marry Dick.

The nearer end of the bar had almost imperceptibly been vacated by drinkers sliding down toward the other end. Pan took the foremost end of the vacated position. He called for drink. As fast as he had drunk, the fiery effects had as swiftly passed away. Yet each drink for the moment kept up that unnatural stimulus.

Pan beckoned for Blinky. That worthy caused a stir, then a silence, by going around the tables, so as not to come between Pan and any men there.

"Blink, do you know where Louise's room is?" queried Pan.

"Shore. Down thish hall . . . third door on left," replied Blinky.

157

"Well, you go over there to Blake and tell him I want to talk to him. Then you go to Louise's room. I'll follow directly."

Blake received the message, but he did not act promptly. Pan caught his suspicious eye, baleful, gleaming. Possibly the man was worse than weak. Presently he left the poker game that he had been watching and shuffled up to Pan. He appeared to be enough under the influence of liquor to be leeringly bold.

"Howdy," he said.

"Blake, today I got from Hardman the truth about the deal you gave me and Lucy," Pan returned, and then in cold deliberate tones he called the man every infamous name known to the ranges. Under this onslaught Blake sank into something akin to abasement.

"Reckon you think," concluded Pan, "that because you're Lucy's father I can't take a shot at you. Don't fool yourself. You've killed her soul . . . and mine. So why shouldn't I kill you? Well, there isn't any reason except that away from Hardman's influence you might brace up. I'll take the chance. You're done in Marco. Jard Hardman is dead, and Dick's chances of seeing the sunrise are mighty thin. Now you rustle out that door and out of Marco. When you make a man of yourself, come to Siccane, Arizona."

Blake lurched himself erect, and met Pan's glance with astonished bewildered eyes, then he wheeled to march out of the saloon.

Pan turned into the hallway leading into the hotel part of the building, and soon encountered Blinky leaning against the wall.

"Blink, isn't she in?" Pan asked, low-voiced and eager.

"Shore, but she won't open the door," replied Blinky.

Pan knocked and called low: "Louise, let us in!"

There was a long wait, then came a low voice: "No."

"Please, it's very important."

"Who are you?"

"It's Panhandle Smith," replied Pan.

"That cowboy's been drinking and I . . . no, I'm sorry."

"Louise, I'm in a bad temper. I ask as a friend. Don't cross me here. I can easily shove in this door."

He heard soft steps, a breathless exclamation, then a key turned in the lock, and the door opened. The lamplight was not bright; Louise stood there half dressed, her bare arms and bosom gleaming. Pan entered, dragging Blinky with him, and closed the door all but tight.

"Louise, it wasn't kind of you to do that," Pan said reproachfully. "Have you any better friends than Blinky or me?"

"Heaven knows . . . I haven't," faltered the girl. "But I've been ill . . . in bed . . . and am just getting out. I . . . I . . . heard about you . . . today . . . and Blink being with you . . . drinking."

Pan stepped to the red-shaded lamp on a small table beside the bed, and turned up the light. The room had more comfort and color than any Pan had seen for many a day.

He bent searching eyes upon Louise. She did look ill—white, with great dark shadows under eyes that glittered with fever, but she seemed really beautiful. What a tragic face it was, betrayed now by lack of paint. Pan had never seen her like this. If he had needed it, this would have warmed his heart to her.

"What do you want of me?" she asked with a nervous twisting of hands she tried to hide.

Pan took her hands and pulled her a little toward him.

"Louise, you like me, don't you, as a friend or a brother?" he asked gently.

159

"Yes, when I'm sober," she replied wanly.

"And you like Blinky, here, don't you . . . like him a lot?"

"I did. I couldn't help it," she returned in the same hopeless tone. "But I hate him when he's drinking, and he hates me when, when. . . ."

"Blink, go out a minute."

The cowboy stared solemnly, then very quietly went out.

"Louise, put something over your shoulders. You'll catch cold. Here," Pan said, and he picked a robe off the bed and wrapped it round her. "I didn't know you were so pretty. No wonder poor Blink worships you."

She drew away from him and sat upon the bed, dark eyes questioning, suspicious. Yet she seemed fascinated. Pan caught a slight quivering of her frame. Where was the audacity, the boldness of this girl? But he did not know her, and he had her word that drink alone enabled her to carry on. He had surprised her. Yet could that account for something different, something quite beyond his power to grasp? Surely this girl could not fear him. Suddenly he remembered that Hardman had fled to this house—was hidden there now. Pan's nerves tautened.

"Louise," he began, taking her hand again, and launching directly into the reason for this interview he had sought, "we've had a great drive. Blink and I have had luck. We sold almost fifteen hundred horses. Well, we're going to Arizona, to a sunny open country, not like this. . . . Now Blink and I want you to go with us."

"What? Go away with you? How, in heaven's name?" she gasped in utter amaze.

"Why, as Blink's wife, of course. And I'll be your big brother," replied Pan, not without agitation. It was a pregnant moment. She stared a second, the mounting fever flushing her white cheeks, her great solemn searching eyes on his. Pan felt strangely embarrassed, yet somehow happy that he had dared to approach her with such a proposition.

Suddenly she kissed him, she buried her face on his shoulder, and he heard her murmur incoherently.

"What do you say, little girl?" he went on. "It's a chance for you to be good again. It'll save that wild cowboy, who never had a decent ambition till he met you. He loves you. He worships you. He hated what you have to suffer here. I'll tell you he. . . ."

"So this is Panhandle Smith?" she interrupted his earnest words, at the same time looking up at him with eyes like dark stars. "No! No! No! I wouldn't degrade even a worthless cowboy."

"You're wrong. He'll not be worthless, if you repay his faith. Louise, don't turn your back on hope, on love, on a home."

"No!" she flashed passionately.

"Why?" he returned in sharp appeal.

"Because he's too good for me. Because I don't deserve your friendship. But I'll love you both all the rest of my miserable life . . . which won't be long."

He took her shaking body in his arms, as if to add force to argument. "But, you poor child, this is no place for you. You'll only ruin yourself . . . commit suicide or be killed in a drunken brawl."

"Panhandle, I may end even worse," she replied in bitter mockery. "I might marry Dick Hardman. He talks of it . . . when he's drinking hard."

Pan released her, and leaned back to see her face. "Marry you! Dick Hardman talks of that?" he burst out incredulously.

"Yes, he does. And I might let him when I'm desperate," she cried.

The girl was now close to the verge of hysteria. Crimson spots glowed in her cheeks, her eyes danced and dilated.

"But, Louise, how can you marry Hardman when he already has a wife?"

She grasped that import only slowly.

"You lie, you gun-slinging cowboy!" she cried wildly.

"No, Louise. He told me so himself."

"He did? When?" she whispered very low.

"Today. He was at the stage office. He meant to leave today. . . . Oh, Louise, I know, I know, because it . . . was . . . my sweetheart . . . he married." Pan ended gaspingly.

"Little Lucy . . . you told me about?"

Pan was confronted now by something terrible.

"Yes, Lucy. I told you," he said, reaching for her. "He forced her to marry him. She thought it was to save her father. Why, Dick paid her father . . . I made him tell me. Yes, Dick Hardman, in his frock coat and high hat! But when I drove him out to get his gun, he forgot that high hat! I killed Matthews. And Louise, I'm going to kill Dick Hardman, too."

"Not you, not you!" she shrieked.

Real delirium now possessed her, and quite beyond knowledge of what she did, the girl leaped swiftly to snatch something from under the pillow of her bed.

Her white arm swept aside red curtains. They hid a shallow closet. It seemed her white shape flashed in and out. A hard choking gasp! Something dropped to the floor with a metallic sound.

The hall door opened with a single sweep. Blinky stood framed there, wild-eyed. And the next instant Dick Hardman staggered from that closet. He had both hands pressed to his side. Blood poured out in a stream. Hardman reeled out into the hall, groaning, to slide down into a widening pool of blood.

It was a paralyzing moment. But Pan recovered first. Snatching a blanket off the bed, he threw it around the girl and lifted her in his arms. At his touch her body relaxed; unconsciousness had come.

"Blink, go ahead," Pan whispered as he went into the hall. "Hurry! Shoot out the lights! Go through the dance hall!"

The cowboy seemed galvanized into action. He leaped over Hardman's body and down the hall, pulling his guns.

Almost immediately thundering shots filled the saloon. *Crash! Crash! Crash!* The lights faded, darkened, went out. Yells and breaking glass, pounding boots merged in a pandemonium of sound.

Pan hurried through the dance hall, found the doorway, gained the side entrance to the street. Blinky waited there, smoking guns in his hands.

"Heah . . . this . . . way," he directed in a panting whisper. Pan followed in the shadow of the houses.

Chapter Eighteen

The street down that way was dark, with but few lights showing. Pan carried Louise at rapid pace, as if she made no burden at all. In the middle of the next block Blinky showed up. They came to an open hallway, dimly lighted. Pan read a sign he remembered. This was the lodging house.

"Go in, Blink," Pan directed quickly. "If you find our parson, chase everybody out but him, and call me *pronto*."

Blinky ran into the place. Pan let Louise down on her feet. She could not stand alone. Although she seemed to be dazedly aware of her surroundings, she was quiet; thus it was evident that she had no remembrance of the recent fateful moments.

Pan thanked God for that. How white the tragic face! Her big eyes resembled bottomless gulfs.

A low whistle made Pan jump. Blinky stood inside, in a flare of light from an open door. He beckoned. Pan lifted the girl and carried her in.

Five minutes later they came out and hurried down the dark street, almost carrying the girl between them. A few people passed, fortunately on the other side. These pedestrians were hurrying in the other direction.

Suddenly Blinky gave Pan a punch. Turning, Pan saw his comrade point back. A dull red flare lighted up the sky. Fire! The Yellow Mine was burning. The crowd of drinkers and gamblers had fled before Blinky's guns, and that must have started the fire. Pan was hoping that only he and Blinky would ever know who had killed Dick Hardman.

The road curved. Soon a dark patch of trees and a flickering light told Pan they had reached his father's place. It gave him a shock. He had forgotten his parents. They entered the lane and cut off through the dew-wet grass of the orchard to the barn. They found three large wagons, and one smaller, with a square canvas top.

Pan got an armful of hay, and, carrying it out to the wagon, he threw it in and spread it out for a bed.

"Reckon we'd better put Louise here," said Pan. "I'll get some blankets from Dad."

He strode toward the house. Although the distance was short, he ran the whole gamut of emotions before he stopped at a lighted window. He heard his father's voice.

"Dad!" he called, tapping on the window. Then he saw his mother and Alice. The door opened with a jerk.

"That you, Pan?" called his father with agitation.

"Nobody else, Dad," replied Pan, trying to calm his voice.

His mother heard and answered with a low cry of relief.

"Dad, come out! Shut that door," Pan said sharply.

Once outside, his father saw the great flare of light above the town.

"Look! What's that? Must be fire!"

"Reckon it is fire," returned Pan shortly. "Blinky shot out the lamps in the Yellow Mine. Fire must have caught from that."

"Yellow Mine?" echoed Smith.

Pan laid a heavy hand on him.

"Lucy! Did she . . . come home?"

"Sure. Didn't you know?"

"What did Lucy tell you?"

"Nothin' much," replied his father in earnest wonder. "She was in an awful state. Said she couldn't go because you were not dead. Poor girl! She had hysterics. But mother got her quieted down by suppertime."

"Dad, does she know?"

"They believed you dead . . . mother an' Lucy. She told how you threw Hardman off of the stage on to the street. Said she almost fainted then. But she come to in time to see you drive him off."

"Is that all she knows?" queried Pan.

"Reckon it is. I know more, but I didn't tell her," replied Smith, lowering his voice to a whisper.

"A-huh!" ejaculated Pan somberly. "Well, better tell Lucy . . . at once . . . that she's a widow."

"Son . . . did . . . did you . . . ?"

"Dad, I didn't kill him," interrupted Pan. "Dick Hardman was . . . was knocked out . . . just before Blinky shot out the lights. Reckon it's a good bet no one will ever know. He sure was burned up in that fire. You needn't tell Lucy that. Just tell her Hardman is dead and that I didn't kill him."

"All right, I'll go right in an' do it," his father replied huskily.

"Before you do, fetch me a roll of blankets. We haven't any beds. And Blinky's wife is with us."

"Wife? I didn't know Blinky had one. Fetch her in."

"No, we've already fixed a place for her in that wagon with the square top," went on Pan. "She's been sick. Rustle, Dad. Fetch me the blankets."

"Got them right inside."

Pan, taking the blankets his father handed him, soon found Blinky exactly as he had left him, leaning over the wagon.

166

"She went right off, asleep, like she was daid," whispered the cowboy, and he stepped up on the wheel hub to lay the blankets softly over the quiet form.

"Come here, cowboy!" called Pan.

And when Blinky got down, Pan laid hold of him with a powerful hand.

"Listen, pard," he began in a low voice, "we're playing a deep game, even though we have to lie. . . . Louise will never remember she cut that traitor's heart out. She was out of her head. If it half returns to her, we'll lie . . . you understand . . . *lie*. Nobody will ever know who did kill Hardman, I'll gamble. I told Dad you'd brought your wife . . . that she'd been sick. He'll tell mother and Lucy. They don't know and they never will know what kind of a girl Louise has been. . . . Savvy, pard?"

"Reckon I do," replied Blinky in hoarse, trembling accents.

Alone now, with the urgent activities past for the time, Pan reverted to the grim and hateful introspection that had haunted his mind.

This once, however, the sinister strife in his soul, that strange icy clutch on his senses—the aftermath of instinctive horror following the death of a man by his hand—wore away before the mounting of a passion that had only waited.

His love for Lucy had not been killed. It lived, it had grown, it was tremendous—and both pity and reason clamored that he be above jealousy and hate. After all, there was excuse for Lucy. She was young, she had been driven by grief over his supposed death and fear for her father. But, oh, the pity of it—of this hard truth against the sweetness of his dream! Life and love were not what he had dreamed them. He must suffer because he had left Lucy to fight her battles.

167

I'll try to forget, he thought to himself. *I've got to. But not yet. I can't do it yet.*

Pan went back to the barn and threw himself upon the hay, where exhausted brain and body sank to sleep and rest. It seemed that a voice and a rude hand tore away the sweet oblivion.

"Pard, are you daid?" came Blinky's voice. "Sunup an' time to rustle."

Pan rose and stretched. His muscles ached as though he had been beaten. How bright the sun! Night was gone, and with it something dreadful.

As they entered the kitchen, Bobby let out a yell and made for him. That loosened a strain for Pan, and he picked up the lad. His mother appeared to be in a blaze of excitement, and at once he realized that all she had needed was his return, safe and sound. Then he heard Alice's voice and Lucy's in reply. The girls entered the kitchen.

Lucy halted in the doorway, with a hand on her breast. Pan's slight inclination, unaccompanied by word of greeting, was as black a pretense as he had ever been guilty of. Sight of her had shot him through and through with pangs of bitter, mocking joy. But he gave no sign. During the meal he did not look at her again.

"Dad, have you got everything we'll need?" Pan queried presently.

"I guess so. I'll help you hitch up," said Bill Smith, following Pan out. "Son, do you look for any trouble this mornin'?"

"Lord, no. I'm not looking for trouble," replied Pan. "I've sure had enough."

"Huh!" ejaculated Blinky. "Your dad means any back fire from Marco. Wal, I say there'll be nothin'. All the same we want to move *pronto*."

168

They had reached the end of the arbor when Lucy's voice called after them: "Pan . . . please wait!"

Lucy came hurriedly, pale, with parted lips, and eyes that held him.

"Mother said you knew, but . . . I must tell you myself," she said brokenly, as she halted close to him. "Day before yesterday . . . those men brought word you'd been . . . killed in a fight over wild horses. It broke my heart. . . . I'd have taken my own life but for my father. I didn't care what happened. . . . Dick pressed me hard. Father begged me to save him from prison. So I . . . I married Dick."

"Yes, I know. I figured it out that way," returned Pan, in strange, thick utterance. "You didn't need to tell me."

"But you . . . you forgive me?" she faltered, reaching to touch him with a shaking hand. How could she look at him like that? How dared she have such love light in her eyes?

"Forgive you for . . . !" he cried in fierce passion. But he could not put into words what she had done. "I meant to kill that dog, Dick Hardman. But I didn't. . . . Forgive you . . . ," he broke off, unable to go on.

Her eyes dilated in horror. With a rending of his heart he swung away and left her.

Presently his father and Blinky hunted him up with news of strong purport plain in their faces.

"Son, Marco is with you to a man!"

"What happened? Out with it."

"Evans drove out bringin' stuff I bought yesterday," returned his father. "He was full as a tick of news. By some miracle, only the Yellow Mine burned. Hardman's body was found burned to a crisp. It was identified by a ring. And his dance-hall girl is probably dead, too. Accordin' to Evans, 'most everybody in Marco wants to shake hands with Panhandle Smith."

169

★ ★ ★ ★ ★

The covered wagons wound slowly down the hill toward Snyder's pasture. The day, in some respects, had been as torturing to Pan as yesterday—but with Marco far behind and the open road ahead, calling, beckoning, the strain began to lessen.

At the pasture gate the drivers halted the wagon teams, waiting for Pan to come up. Gus had opened the wide-barred gate, and now stood there with a grin of relief and gladness.

"Drive in!" shouted Pan from behind. "We'll camp here tonight."

He walked out to take a look at the horses, which were scattered on the far side of the pasture. They were not nearly so wild as he had expected them to be. The saddle and wagon horses grazed among them. Sight of Little Bay brought keen pain to Pan.

Presently there came the call to supper, which had been laid upon a new tarpaulin spread on the ground. The men flopped down, and sat cross-legged, each with silent or vociferous appreciation of that generous repast.

It was after nightfall when Pan heard Blinky's call. He hurried over to the wagon, where he found his comrade tremendously excited.

"Pard, she's waked up," he whispered. Pan strode to the wagon.

"Hello, Louise," he said gently.

"Where am I?" she replied huskily.

"On the way to Arizona."

"I've been sick?" she queried.

"Reckon you have . . . a little," replied Pan.

"And you boys have kidnapped me?"

"I'm afraid that's so, Louise."

"Get me some water! My head's bursting. And help me out of this haymow."

Pan lifted her out of the wagon. Then he ran off toward camp to get water. Upon returning, he found Blinky trying to put a blanket around Louise's shoulders. She threw it off.

"Wait till I cool off," she said. "I'm shaky, all right. Thanks, Panhandle, for the drink."

They lifted her back into the wagon and covered her. In the pale starlight her eyes looked unnaturally big and black.

"No use . . . to lie," she said drowsily. "I'm glad to leave . . . Marco. Take me anywhere."

They found the campfire deserted except for Gus and Pan's father. Evidently Pan's advent interrupted a story that had been most exciting to Gus.

"Son, I . . . I was just tellin' Gus all I know about what come off yesterday," explained Bill Smith with some haste. "You come mighty near buttin' right into the weddin'!"

Pan, whose back had been turned to the campfire light, suddenly whirled.

"What?" he cried. Then there seemed to be a cessation of all his faculties.

"Why, Son, you needn't jump out of your boots," returned the father, somewhat offended. "Lucy was married to Hardman in the stage office just before you got there. Now, I was only sayin' how funny it'd been if you had got there sooner."

"I had an idea . . . she'd been married . . . days," Pan replied in a queer, strangled voice.

Without another word he stalked away into the darkness. The shock of incredulous amaze passed away, leaving him in the grip of joy and gratitude and remorse.

Chapter Nineteen

It was Pan who routed out the campers next morning when the first rose of dawn flushed the clear-cut horizon line.

He had the firewood collected and the saddle horses in for their grain before Blinky presented himself.

"Pard," he whispered huskily, "the cyclone's busted."

"Yes?" queried Pan.

"I was pullin' on my boots when Louise pokes her head above the wagon an' says . . . 'Hey, you bowlegged gurl-snatcher, where's my clothes?'

" 'Louise,' I says, 'we shore forgot them, an' they burned up with all the rest of the Yellow Mine. An' if you want to know, my dear, I'm darn' glad of it.'

"Then, Pan, she began to swear at me, an' I jumps up mad, but right dignified, an' says . . . 'Missus Somers, I'll require you to stop usin' profanity.'

"She gave a gasp an' fell back in the wagon. An' you bet I run fer you. Now, pard, for heaven's sake, what'll I do?"

"Cowboy, you've done noble," replied Pan. "I swear I can fix it up with Louise. I swear I can fix anything."

Whereupon he hurried over to the campfire, where he found Lucy, a mass of golden hair hanging down her back, to which she was vigorously applying a brush.

"Hello, Lucy," he said coolly.

"Oh . . . how you startled . . . me!" she exclaimed, turning with a blush.

"Say, won't you help us out?" he went on, not so coolly. "The other night, in the excitement, we forgot to fetch Louise's clothes. Fact is, we grabbed her up out of a sick bed, with only a dressing gown and a blanket. Won't you lend her some clothes, shoes, stockings . . . and . . . everything?"

"Indeed, I will," responded Lucy, and she climbed into the covered wagon.

Pan waited, and presently began to pace to and fro. He was restless, eager, buoyant. He could not stand still.

"Here, Pan!" Lucy called, reappearing with a large bundle. "Here's all she'll need, I think. It was lucky we bought new things. Alice and I can get along with one mirror, brush, and comb."

"Thanks," he said. "It was lucky. Sure our luck has changed."

"Don't forget some water," Lucy added practically, calling after him.

Thus burdened, Pan hurried back to Louise's wagon and deposited the basin on the seat, and the bundle beside her. "There you are," he said cheerily.

"Come on, Blink!" he called to the cowboy watching from behind the trees. "Let's wrangle the teams."

"Gus an' your dad are comin' in with them now," replied Blinky.

At this juncture they were called to breakfast. It seemed to Pan that the bursting sun knew the dark world had been transformed to a shining one. Yet he played with his happiness like a cat with a mouse.

When he presented himself before Louise, he scarcely recognized her in the prim, comely change of apparel. The atmosphere of the Yellow Mine had vanished. She had managed to eat some breakfast that Blinky brought. Blinky discreetly found a task that took him away.

"We've a little time to talk now, Louise," said Pan. He led her under the cottonwoods to the pasture fence, where he found a seat for her.

"Pan, why did you do this thing?" she asked.

"Because my friend loves you, and you told me you tried to keep him away from you . . . that, if you didn't, you would like him too well," answered Pan. "I thought here's an opportunity to make a man out of my friend, and save the soul of a girl who hasn't had a chance. So I planned it and did it."

"But, Pan . . . I'm no fit wife for him."

"You can be," went on Pan with strong feeling. "Just blot out the past. Begin now. Blink will make a good man, a successful rancher. He has money enough to start with. He'll never drink again. No matter what you call yourself, you're the only girl he ever loved. Could you come to love my friend . . . in time . . . I mean? That's the great thing."

"I believe I love him now," she murmured. "That's why I can't risk it. Someone who knew me would turn up. To disgrace my husband and children, if I had any."

"Not one chance in a million," flashed Pan. "We're going far . . . into another country. . . . Besides, everyone in Marco believes you lost your life in the fire."

"What . . . fire?"

"The Yellow Mine burned. It must have caught . . . when we shot out the lamps. . . . Dick Hardman was burned, and they figured you died, too."

Louise leaped up, ghastly pale.

"I remember now. . . . Blink came to my room," she said hoarsely. "I wouldn't let him in. Then you came. . . . Oh, I remember now. I let you in when Dick Hardman was hiding in my closet."

174

"I knew you had him hidden."

"You meant to kill him! He came to me when I was sick in bed. He begged me to hide him. And I did. . . . Then you talked to me, as you're talking now. . . . It isn't all clear because I must have been out of my head."

"Louise, what did I tell you about Hardman?" returned Pan. "I told you Hardman had forced my sweetheart, Lucy, to marry him."

"What? He did that?"

"Reckon he did. I got there too late. But I drove him off to get a gun. Then he hid there with you."

"So that was why?" she pondered, as if trying to penetrate the cloudiness of her mind. "Some of it comes back like a horrible dream."

"Sure," he hurried on. "Let me get it over. I told you he couldn't marry you when he already had a wife. You went crazy then. Hardman came rushing out of the closet. Pretty nasty, he was, Louise. Well, I left him lying in the hall! I grabbed you . . . wrapped you in a blanket . . . and ran out. Blink was waiting. He shot out the lights in the saloon. We got away. The place burned up . . . and Hardman. . . ."

"Oh, heaven! Burned alive?"

"No," replied Pan hoarsely.

"Pan . . . you . . . you avenged me . . . and your Lucy . . . you . . . ?" she whispered.

"Hush! Don't speak it! Don't ever think it again," he said sternly. "That's our secret. Rumor has it he fled from me to hide with you, and probably you both burned up."

"But Lucy . . . your mother!" she cried.

"They know nothing except that you're my friend's wife . . . that you've been ill," he replied. "They're all kindness and sympathy. Play your part now, Louise. You and Blink make up your past. Just a few simple statements. Then bury the past forever."

"Oh . . . I'm slipping . . . slipping . . . ," she whispered, bursting into tears. "Help me . . . back to the wagon."

She walked a few rods with Pan's arm supporting her. Then she collapsed. He had to carry her to the wagon. Then he espied Blinky, coming in manifest concern.

"Pard," said Pan in his ear, "you've a pat hand. Play it for all you're worth."

The wagons rolled down the long winding open road.

For the shortest, fullest eight hours Pan had ever experienced he matched his wits against the wild horses that he and Gus had to drive. It was a downgrade, and the wagons rolled thirty miles before Pan picked a camp site in the mouth of a little grassy cañon where the wild horses could be corralled. Jack rabbits, deer, coyotes ranged away from the noisy invasion of their solitude. It was wild country. Marco was a distant forty miles up the sweeping ranges—far behind—gone into the past.

Four days on the way to Siccane! So far Pan had carried on his pretense of aloofness from Lucy, apparently blind to the wondering appeal in her eyes. Long ago he had forgiven her. Yet he waited, divining surely that some day or night, when an opportune moment came, she would voice the question in her eyes.

That very evening, when he went to fetch water, she waylaid him.

"Panhandle Smith, you are killing me!" she said with great eyes of accusation.

"How so?" he asked weakly.

"You know," she retorted, "and I won't stand it any longer."

"What is it you won't stand?"

But suddenly Lucy broke down. "Don't. Don't keep it up!" she cried desperately. "I love only you. All my life it's been only you."

"Lucy! Tomorrow we ride into Green River. Will you marry me there?"

"Yes . . . if you . . . love me," she whispered, going close to him.

Arizona land! It was not only a far country attained, but another, strange and beautiful. Siccane lay a white-and-green dot far over the purple sage. The golden-walled mesas stood up, black-fringed against the blue. In the bold notches burned the red of autumn foliage. Valleys spread between the tablelands. There was room for a hundred homesteads.

"Water! Grass! No fences!" Pan's father exclaimed with a glad note of renewed youth.

"Dad . . . Lucy . . . look," Pan replied, pointing across the valley. "See that first big notch in the wall. Thick with bright green. There's water. And see the open cañon with the cedars scattered? What a place for a ranch! It has been waiting for us all these years. That's where we'll homestead."

"Wal, pard, an' you, Louise . . . look over heah a ways," drawled Blinky, with long arm outstretched. "See the red circle wall, with the brook shinin' down like a ribbon. Lookin' to the south? Warm in winter . . . cool in summer. Thet's the homestead for us."

The wagons rolled on behind wild horses that needed little driving. On into the rich grass where no wheel track showed—on into the sage toward the beckoning walls.

About the Author

Zane Grey was born Pearl Zane Gray at Zanesville, Ohio in 1872. He was graduated from the University of Pennsylvania in 1896 with a degree in dentistry. He practiced in New York City while striving to make a living by writing. He married Lina Elise Roth in 1905 and with her financial assistance he published his first novel himself, BETTY ZANE (1903). Closing his dental office, the Greys moved into a cottage on the Delaware River, near Lackawaxen, Pennsylvania. Grey took his first trip to Arizona in 1907 and, following his return, wrote THE HERITAGE OF THE DESERT (1910). The profound effect that the desert had had on him was so vibrantly captured that it still comes alive for a reader. Grey couldn't have been more fortunate in his choice of a mate. Trained in English at Hunter College, Lina Grey proofread every manuscript Grey wrote, polished his prose, and she effectively managed their financial affairs. Grey's early novels were serialized in pulp magazines, but by 1918 he had graduated to the slick magazine market. Motion picture rights brought in a fortune and, with 109 films based on his work, Grey set a record yet to be equaled by any other author. Zane Grey was not a realistic writer, but rather one who charted the interiors of the soul through encounters with the wilderness. He provided characters no more realistic than one finds in Balzac, Dickens, or Thomas Mann, but nonetheless they have a vital story to tell. "There was so much unexpressed feeling that could not be entirely portrayed," Loren Grey, Grey's younger son and a noted psychologist, once recalled, "that, in later years, he would weep when re-reading one of his own books." More than stories, Grey fashioned psychodramas about the odyssey of the human soul. They may not be the stuff of the real world, but without them the real world has no meaning—which may go a long way to explain the hold he has had on an enraptured reading public ever since his first Western romance in 1910. His next **Five Star Western** will be THE DESERT CRUCIBLE.